The Purple House

Steven Freeman

A Bright Pen Book

Copyright © Steven Freeman 2011

Cover design by Jim Tyson ©

All Rights reserved. No part of this publication may be reproduced, stored in a retrieval system, or transmitted, in any form or by any means, electronic, mechanical, photocopy, recording or otherwise, without prior written permission of the copyright owner. Nor can it be circulated in any form of binding or cover other than that in which it is published and without similar condition including this condition being imposed on a subsequent purchaser.

British Library Cataloguing in Publication Data.
A catalogue record for this book is available from the British Library.

ISBN 978 0 7552 1364 1

Authors OnLine Ltd
19 The Cinques
Gamlingay, Sandy
Bedfordshire SG19 3NU
England

This book is also available in e-book format, details of which are available at www.authorsonline.co.uk

The Purple House

By the same author

Black Sail

To the memory of Varya Vee

and to all those who knew

and loved the Purple House

These novels will give way, by and by, to diaries or autobiographies – captivating books, if only a man knew how to choose among what he calls his experiences, and how to record truth truly.

Ralph Waldo Emerson

Contents

PART ONE

the way of the word 13

more fully human 19

the unreasonable man 26

want to live my life! 30

in this real world 34

skid row in the fells 39

the vagabond writer 44

responsibility of a writer 47

a kindred spirit 54

PART TWO

a beautiful morning 61

quickly and naturally 69

provided providentially 73

play the game 75

naked and vulnerable 78

this is the life *81*

the market place *86*

too much information? *90*

essence of the life-force *96*

check on! *100*

winning me over *109*

in the boiler room *118*

don't worry, be happy *121*

up in the clouds *128*

a sort of mandala *133*

comrades in arms *136*

we all need a home *143*

flesh and blood *147*

worms in the water *153*

my home entertainment *157*

on the treadmill *164*

recreating my world *167*

just a quickie *172*

a literary event *176*

the real work *178*

PART THREE

make soup, not war *183*

unfit for human habitation *189*

coming through *196*

the bohemian nature *201*

our little dinner party *206*

what a madhouse! *211*

the 'living' room *213*

the face of the devil *216*

the dharma bums *219*

the men in the white coats *222*

where is home? *225*

what is rent? *231*

might go feral *233*

things just happen *236*

no man is an island *242*

the stuff of life *248*

your way, my way, the way *254*

PART ONE

the way of the word

Once there was a purple house that stood beside the road in the Newlands Valley, about halfway between Keswick and Buttermere. It was situated by a hairpin bend at the foot of the steeply-sloping Causey Pike, where a bridge crosses a stream, Rigg Beck – after which the house was named. It was a large wooden building, weird-looking, like something out of a fairy tale or a horror movie, and painted – of course – the colour purple.

I first moved into the house in the summer of '93 with the purpose of writing a novel. I had been living in Keswick and working in the kitchen of a vegetarian restaurant, but I felt the time had come to retreat from the world and devote myself to my creative 'mission'. The idea of writing a novel had seriously taken hold of me about a year prior to this, when I was living in Carlisle. I had made numerous starts and lots of notes. I had the whole thing planned out, but found I couldn't get going with it whilst I was busy working at the restaurant. I felt the only way to do it was to take time out and fully immerse myself in the thing. This meant giving up my job and going to live somewhere really quiet, where I could finally get on with it. It was a precarious step to be sure, but I was no stranger to living precariously. Most of the previous five years of my life had been singularly precarious – with much moving around, changing addresses and jobs, at times unemployed, at times homeless and virtually penniless. One of the things that kept me going was the desire, the *need* to be creative, both in writing, and in my life itself. I was on some kind of spiritual quest. I had read Jack Kerouac's 'The Dharma Bums' and, although not a Buddhist, I saw myself as a sort of 'dharma bum'. And The Way for me was to be through The Word, which is to say *literature*, and particularly the *novel*.

In Keswick I had been living in a very small flat in the basement of a house on the outskirts of town. It wasn't the right place to get my creativity flowing. It was a big modern house on a middle-class estate. To me it felt soulless. The deal with the landlady was that I would do a few hours gardening a week in return for a low rent on the flat. I remember cutting the grass on the front lawn, which she wanted to keep really neat and tidy – with no dandelions or suchlike showing their faces. This seemed symbolic of the mentality of those who lived on the estate – uptight, small-minded and mean-spirited. Strangely she had been interested in buying the Purple House a couple of years prior to this – so she told me. Thankfully it never happened. If it had she would no doubt have 'improved' it and converted it into something with a completely different vibe. That was the thing – the *vibe*. I found the vibe on this estate to be depressing – soul-crushing even. It may have been a 'nice' area, but it felt sterile to me. Also the flat was claustrophobic with low ceilings and the sound of the landlady and her teenaged children clomping around on the floor above me. I felt trapped in a hole, and I needed to escape. I needed space – space to be free, to grow and be vital. I needed to be somewhere alternative, somewhere out of town, somewhere away from the petty bourgeois culture, somewhere in the fells, somewhere peaceful, and somewhere *cheap*. The Purple House seemed to be the perfect place.

The Purple House was properly known as 'Rigg Beck', although some people called it 'Big Wreck'. It was in a poor state of repair, with some windows broken, and the woodwork going rotten. It was slowly 'falling down' and it was a slightly scary-looking place, but it was also a magnificent ramshackle palace in the fells, where you could rent a room cheaply from the eccentric landlady, Mrs Varya Vee. I got hold of her phone number and arranged to meet her to talk about renting a room. I walked up the valley on a beautiful spring morning and arrived at the house at the appointed time. And there she was, sitting on a bench on the roadside verandah, a plump bespectacled figure wearing a scruffy purple fleece jacket, and sunning herself like a cat. I walked up to her and introduced myself. 'Pleased to meet you' she said. 'Do come in and I'll make a pot of tea' – all very polite and terribly well-spoken. She smiled at me and raised herself awkwardly from the bench. She was in her seventies and not as mobile as she used to be. We went down into the basement, which was her own self-contained flat, and she made some tea and we sat down and talked – or rather *she* talked and I listened. She talked too much, but I suppose she got a bit lonely living at the house on her own, and she liked to talk to people when she got the chance.

She told me that she had long since separated from her husband, and her numerous children had all grown up and left the place a good few years ago. The children came to visit her from time to time, and she had friends in the valley and in town who visited her and gave her lifts for shopping or whatever. She talked for an hour or so, mainly about the house and her many previous lodgers and visitors. Apparently a number of famous writers had stayed there in years gone by. It was a place that attracted creative people, especially writers and painters, as well as all kinds of unconventional types – hippies, dropouts, 'escapees'. In the sixties and seventies the house had been a very busy sort of alternative hostel. In those days she used to place an advert for accommodation headed 'LOVERS OF THE WORLD UNITE' in the classified section of The New Statesman. But times had changed, the famous Purple House was no longer popular, and the building had deteriorated. There were five or six rooms that were habitable, and a few more on the top floor which she didn't let out because of fire regulations.

We went upstairs to the first floor and she showed me round. The communal kitchen was very dirty and untidy, having been left in a mess ever since the departure of the last tenants at the back end of the last season. The bathroom was dark and dingy, with a heavily-stained bath, a cracked toilet seat, and an old black and white poster of Marilyn Monroe on the wall. Some of the bedrooms were quite large and self-contained, with fridges and cookers and armchairs. Mrs Vee suggested that I take the 'Red Room', and this was probably the best one by virtue of its size, furniture and back-of-house position – with eastward aspect over the garden and towards the ridge of Cat Bells on the other side of the valley. The furniture included a bed, wardrobe, bookshelves, two armchairs, sink, fridge, cupboards, and a large solid desk by the east-facing window. The walls were magnolia rather than red, but there was a red plastic lampshade hanging from the ceiling.

I told Mrs Vee that I was a writer and that I was planning to write a novel here. She approved of that, but was concerned about my lack of a job, and whether or not I would be able to afford to pay the rent. I paid her for two weeks (in those days it was probably about £30 a week). She told me that the Red Room was a good room for writing. It was the room where none other than Ted Hughes had once stayed for a few weeks back in 1962. He'd gone to live there with his new girlfriend, Assia Wevill, after Sylvia Plath killed herself. More recently it was the room where Mack, the then warden of Black Sail, had lived the previous season. And I suppose the Purple House was the sort of place that would attract the sort of person who would also be attracted to living at Black Sail. Anyway, it seemed like the Red Room was the best room in the house. And, for the time being at least, I was going to be the only lodger – which suited me just fine, as I wanted solitude, peace and quiet.

more fully human

So I installed myself in the Red Room and soon set to work on writing 'Communion'. I sat at the desk and wrote my 'novel', composing by hand in the mornings, and typing it up in the afternoons. It began with a character based on myself who is fed up of his job at a 'computer centre' and he leaves for the 'Nature Park' in search of a happier, more meaningful way of life...

As the train pulled out of the station I looked out of the window. Government office blocks of concrete and mirrored glass stood tall and arrogant against the fast-moving dark-grey clouds of a winter sky. And I looked back on my life at the computer centre – the life I was leaving behind.

For too long I had sat at a computer terminal, trying to find the errors of logic in my programs. I can't believe that that they took me on, and I can't believe that I applied for it because I certainly wasn't cut out for it. I didn't have the right sort of mind for the job, and I didn't have the right sort of attitude for the way of life that went with it. They actually told me that I was a square peg trying to fit into a round hole and – much as I tried to force it – I didn't fit in. It seemed that my life itself had been getting to be like a program, that I was allowing myself to be programmed and that I was even collaborating in this self-programming. But who had designed this program? It wasn't me – that's for sure.

For a long time I had been unhappy, but I hadn't really known what to do about it. I had allowed myself to become trapped – trapped into a particular way of thinking, trapped into a particular way of being. And all my efforts to develop an aptitude for the work and for the way of life that went with it were going against my own grain. It was like I was trying to solve errors of logic in my own life-program, when really the problem was not so much in the logic as in the premises and values within which the logic was framed. Do you know what I mean? It was the framework itself that made no sense. It was all very well having a steady career job with a good salary, pension scheme, holidays and all the rest of it, but the job, the town, the way of life – it all seemed soulless somehow. And to have carried on there I would have been selling my soul for a kind of automated existence that wasn't quite human. But what did it mean to be human anyway? I wasn't quite sure, but I knew that I didn't feel as human as I wanted to be. And I suppose that was my quest – to be more fully human (or less human, if being human meant leading a normal life). I felt that I had potential for living a life that was more full, more vital, more spiritual.

So how was I going to realise this potential? How was I going to be more (or less) human? Well I hoped that I might find what I needed living among the hills, closer to Nature and away from mainstream programmed society. Also I hoped that I would find work that was more meaningful to me, something that I could believe in. And so one day in March I found myself on a train heading northwards to the Lakes and on my way to a new way of life. Earlier that afternoon I had handed in my identity tag at the computer centre, and I felt that the old me no longer existed – he had to die in order that the new me could be born.

Pausing to look out of the window I see the tiny figures of walkers slowly moving along the ridge of Cat Bells on the other side of the valley. It's a beautiful summer's morning. My mind is still and I'm feeling serene, alert, alive. It's the effect of writing. But I want to feel physically alive too, and to feel the sun on my body. I'll get out there for a run in a little while, but I'll do a bit more writing first... But now I'm distracted by a martin swooping out of the air and flying into the eaves just above the window, where there's a nest. I hear the twittering of the young ones. I get up from my chair and crane my neck to get a better look and I see three baby birds craning their necks towards their mother, who has brought them food. And then I look down into the garden, where I see Mrs

Vee ambling among the flowers. It's what you might call a 'wild' garden, which is to say it isn't overly orderly or 'managed' – and I like it that way. There's a big old stone fountain among the plants, which adds an element of grandness to the scene. A white cat lazily follows Mrs Vee and brushes against her leg. I decide to break off from the writing, and get myself ready for a run.

I tidy up my papers on the desk, and then walk over to the other side of the room, where my radio-cassette 'ghetto blaster' sits on one of the shelves. I select a cassette from my collection, a compilation of Dead Can Dance tracks that a friend taped for me. I've been listening to this tape a lot recently. It sort of goes with my serious novel-writing mode, and it goes with this room and this house. The first track that comes on is *Anywhere Out Of This World*. After a slow-building intro the song gets going, like an epic piece of classical music, measured, dramatic and profound. Next up is *Black Sun*, still very dramatic, but this time moving along at a faster pace, the timpani drumming beating out a rhythm more conducive to preparing for a run. Brendan Perry's strong singing of dark pessimistic words is strangely uplifting. Trombones are blaring as I change into my running shorts and do some stretching exercises, then a few press-ups and sit-ups. And then I pick up my Walsh running shoes by the door, put some coins in the electricity meter on the landing and switch the immersion heater on in the bathroom. I walk barefoot down the dusty old stair carpet, past an old poster of a young and beautiful Kate Bush pouting at me, and across the tiled hallway to the massive front door (which is never locked). And

I sit on the purple-painted wooden bench on the verandah to put my socks and fell shoes on. It's a beautiful sunny day, and this is an idyllic spot. A car going past slows down momentarily and the woman on the passenger side gazes at the house, then smiles and waves at me. I get up from the bench and walk down the lane at the side of the house, past the little red post-box on the right, then breaking into a jog, down the road to the bridge over Newlands Beck, then branching off up the track past Newlands Church, and the adjoining old schoolhouse – where Mrs Vee's children would have gone to school. Getting into a steady rhythm now as I plod up this track, through Low Snab farmyard, through a gate (on which there is an old yellow sign – 'SHUT THIS GATE AND USE COOPERS DIP'), turn right, then I'm onto the lower slopes of the fell, looking at the spoil heaps of old mine workings – where they mined for lead mainly, but also *gold*, one of the mines being called 'Goldscope'. (And there's a lad who works at Sundance Wholefoods in Keswick who used to live at Rigg Beck, and he told me he came out here the other week, panning for gold, though without any success.) Anyway, it's a change of gradient now as the climb up onto the ridge begins, and it's a mixture of running and walking, and even a bit of scrambling on the rocky bits. It's hard work, and I'm sweating in the heat of the sun, so I take my tee-shirt off and stuff it into my bum bag. I feel more free with my top off – like a wild animal just enjoying running around his habitat, feeling the warmth of the sun on his face and chest. And it inspires me to pick up the pace and find another 'gear'. It's a steep pull up onto the summit, but then it's a beautiful fast running descent down and round Hindscarth Edge, with a fantastic view of High Crag and Fleetwith Pike. Then it's a steady climb up onto Dale Head, taking a narrow trod skirting below the main path, through some crags and with an exciting view down the steep drop to the Honister Pass road. At the top of Dale Head I pause momentarily to say 'hello' to some walkers who stand close to the tall round cairn and ask me where I'm going. Then I drop off down to Dalehead Tarn, keeping to the right of the main path, a steep, difficult jarring descent, but I manage to keep the rhythm going, then cross the beck at the bottom, then start the steady climb up onto High Spy. I manage to keep running up here, and I'm feeling strong, the midday sun on my back now, my legs and arms pumping, working hard, breathing hard but regular, in control, focussed. Emerging at High Spy, there's another tall round carefully-constructed cairn – with a young couple, the man taking a photograph of his girlfriend by the cairn. And I drop down to the right of the main path, following a faint trod, meandering round in a short cut to pick up the main path later. It's very fast running along the Maiden Moor ridge and it feels like I'm flying as I pass lots of walkers coming the other way. Then I take another little short cut, through the grass, before the exciting drop down to Hause Gate, taking little trods through the heather to the right of the main path, running and jumping and throwing myself downwards, concentrating hard on the ground beneath my feet until I arrive at the col called Hause Gate, where I pause for a moment, wondering whether to carry on and up Cat Bells, but deciding to leave it out because it takes me a little out of my way and there are hordes of people up there. So I drop off to my left on a grassy path that becomes rocky and crosses a stream and then finally brings me out at the hamlet of Little Town. From here it's a jog down the road to Chapel Bridge, then back up the road to the house. And as I'm jogging down the road with a view of Hindscarth and Robinson dead ahead I'm thinking how beautiful this valley is. It has a sort of fairy tale beauty with these fells rearing up steeply on all sides, enclosing and embracing the lush green wooded valley, white-washed farmhouses dotted here and there, Herdwick lambs jumping around the fields, their mothers smiling – as they usually do. This is surely paradise. And I'm smiling myself as I jog down the road, past all the cars parked at the bottom, over the bridge and back up to the road, my legs feeling tired now, the house coming into view, surrounded by mature trees, overlooked by heather-clad Causey Pike, and blending well into the landscape (blending better in fact than those white-washed farmhouses.)

And when I finally arrive back at the house Mrs Vee is sitting on the bench on the verandah. 'Sol' she says, 'did you have a good run?' I feel like I should put my tee-shirt on in her presence, but I decide not to bother. She's not used to having fellrunners staying at the house and I think she thinks fell-running is a bit crazy – which I suppose it is – but she *is* used to having all sorts of eccentric people stay at the house, so it doesn't matter. We remark on what a beautiful day it is, but I don't want to get waylaid with one of her monologues, so I go in and get myself a bath, the face of Marilyn Monroe looking down on me. Apparently one of the previous tenants was a big fan.

the unreasonable man

Having had my bath I get changed and get some bits and pieces for lunch from the fridge in my room – a loaf, a tub of margarine, cottage cheese and a lettuce. And then I go into the kitchen – a ragged little room with a bare wooden floor, a big solid wooden table, a few hard chairs, peeling 70s flowery wallpaper, an old electric cooker, an ironing board propped against the wall (not that Rigg Beck-types tend to be ironing-types), some shelves with an assortment of pots, pans, cutlery and my food store, and a sink and draining board with its usual sprinkling of mouse-droppings. It's a scruffy room that has seen better days, but it's functional and it's light – especially on a sunny day like today with the sunshine pouring through the windows. 'Be not sad; shine like the noonday sun.'

And I make my lunch of cottage cheese and lettuce sandwiches on Bryson's sunflower wholemeal bread, and I sit down at the big oak table and flip through *The Keswick Reminder*. 'Registered as a newspaper' it says on the front page, and 'Price 15p'. It looks very old-fashioned with its narrow columns of tiny newsprint under bold headings of 'LOCAL ARRESTS', 'KESWICK PHILATELIC SOCIETY', 'ONIONS STOLEN FROM ALLOTMENT', 'KESWICK BRIDGE CLUB', 'THE WEATHER IN MAY' (a statistical analysis of last month's weather), and incredibly long sports reports for the rugby club and the football club. Mingled in with the news there are adverts for restaurants, estate agents, holiday cottage companies, garages, cinema listings, and a few job adverts. It's more like a parish newsletter than a newspaper and its ten pages can be skim-read in less than five minutes. And I skim quickly through most of it, slowing down to read the book review section... There are reviews of yet another walking guide to the Lakes, and one about steam trains of yesteryear. Neither book interests me, but I read the reviews anyway, trying to imagine what it would be like to read a review of my own book here. The writing comes across as having been written by someone quite old and very conservative – which reflects the Keswick demographic. And I wonder what kind of reception my book would get from this reviewer, and from 'the good people' of Keswick. I suspect not a sympathetic one. And most Keswickians probably consider Rigg Beck to be a blot on the landscape, and all those associated with it as being in some way suspect, or at least not 'respectable'.

I turn to the back page for the classified ads – the most interesting bit. There are more 'SITUATIONS VACANT', and I notice that there is a job going at a cafe in town called 'The Honeypot'. I also look at the 'MOTORS FOR SALE' and dream about owning a car again. And I look at the 'TO LET' section and dream about my own self-contained place, but the rents are way too high – besides which I am behind with my rent here at Rigg Beck, and I have no means of raising a deposit. I fold the paper and leave it on the table, and put the kettle on to make a peppermint tea. And as I wait for the kettle to boil I walk over to the window and look at the sheep in the field over the road – some of them grazing, others lazing and sunbathing. And then I look out the other window, which overlooks the garden, and see Mrs Vee reading a book and drinking tea. I make my own tea and then go back to the Red Room to write.

This afternoon I'll type up the hand-written composing that I did this morning. I sit at the desk and look at what I've written, then make a start...My typing is slow and awkward at first – it takes me a while to get into it, but gradually my fingers speed up and my key-pressing becomes more accurate. It's an old portable typewriter. There's no correction ribbon and so when I make a mistake I have to go back and use slips of *Tippex* paper, or else I just type a line through a wrong letter or word. It's a laborious task, but I'm determined to get this first draft typescript as 'clean' as possible. At the corner of the desk, next to my plastic pen and pencil holder and my mug of peppermint tea sitting on a beer mat, there is a square yellow *Post-it* on which I have written a quote from

George Bernard Shaw's *Man and Superman*: '*The reasonable man adapts himself to the world; the unreasonable one persists in trying to adapt the world to himself. Therefore all progress depends on the unreasonable man.*'

want to live my life!

I'd been spending too much time on my own, and when my friend Mark from Carlisle came to visit me I'd almost forgotten how to have a conversation. Initially I was pleased to see him and grateful for his company, but at the same time I felt that my solitude had been violated and that we didn't have much to talk about. I felt that I'd grown apart from him. Also I felt that he didn't understand what I was trying to achieve with my book. Mark was basically a sensible middle-class middle-of-the road sort of a bloke, and he couldn't see why I wanted to devote myself to writing. And I think he thought I was a bit crazy for jacking in my job at the restaurant. In Mark's opinion art was something you did as a hobby in your spare time after work. We ended up having a bit of an argument about this. I remember Mark saying something about Maslow's 'hierarchy of needs', and how I should get myself a steadier, more secure sort of life before embarking on some major project of self-actualisation. And I replied that Maslow's system didn't apply to me because self-actualisation was much more than just the top of the pyramid, the icing on the cake, it was *everything* to me. And then I switched a bit and said that it wasn't actually my *self* that I was trying to actualise – it was my *novel*. And I quoted Jung: 'Art is a kind of innate drive that seizes a human being and makes him its instrument. The artist is not a person endowed with free will who seeks his own ends, but one who allows art to realise its purpose through him.'

Mark left and I went for a run. I felt a bit threatened by him – or rather by the world he stood for. Maybe he was right, and maybe I was crazy and deluded. I consulted Nietzsche, finding sympathetic encouragement in *Thus Spoke Zarathustra*, 'Of the Way of the Creator'. Yes, I had wanted to go apart and be alone. But the voice of the herd (Mark) was ringing in me. I had escaped from the yoke of the restaurant, but ought I to have done so? Yes! I was strong, I had my ruling idea, I was going the way to myself which led past myself, and yes, I was prepared to burn myself in my own flame in order to become new. It seemed that my only friend was Nietzsche. Perhaps, like him, I would go insane. Perhaps I already *was* insane. (I didn't care, as long as I got my novel written and published.) Or perhaps – as Sharon later put it to me – 'You're in danger of disappearing up your own arse!'

At this point I should introduce you to Sharon, with whom I worked at the restaurant. She was the main cook there and I was her assistant – that is until she suddenly left and I ended up being the main cook. She was a tall, slim, dark-haired girl in her early twenties, a bit hippyish I suppose, and with a fondness for wearing red clothing (when she wasn't in her kitchen whites). 'Sharon' wasn't her given name but the name she had chosen for herself – perhaps to try and distance herself from her middle-class upbringing, and the middle-class name that went with it. She also had a Sanskrit name – which she'd been given whilst staying on Osho's commune in India (hence her taste for red clothing), but she only used that one with her *sannyassin* friends. Anyway, she was good fun to work with – down-to-earth, open and straightforward. She was always giving me hugs and I wasn't sure if she fancied me but, although we got on well together, the sexual chemistry somehow just wasn't there so we remained just friends.

She used to get stressed-out at the restaurant – which was more of a cafe or tea shop by day – when it got busy, and she'd suddenly disappear upstairs for a meditation break, and leave me in charge, on my own. Upstairs there were some letting rooms and a guests' lounge, because it was a guest house as well as a tea shop/restaurant. (From now on I'm just going to refer to the place as 'the tea shop' – which in fact is what everybody called it.) Anyway, Sharon would go to the lounge to meditate or to read one of her books by Osho. Sometimes she went out the back of the kitchen, where she'd sit in the sun on an oil drum, motionless, staring into space. Some passers-by no doubt wondered what was wrong with this chef, who was apparently in some kind of trance. 'She's mebbe had enough...working at that spot has done 'er 'ead in.'

And she *had* had enough. One day, just before Easter, she gave in her week's notice to the boss, Chris, declaring that 'I want to *live* my life!' She'd come to an arrangement with Chris such that he'd tell the dole office that her job had just been a temporary contract, once they made their enquiries. She'd be able to claim benefits and lead a life of leisure for the summer – lucky Sharon.

As for me, I became employed in a full-time capacity and stepped into Sharon's shoes as the main daytime cook. And it was usually very busy from start to finish – chopping, chopping and more chopping of vegetables, endless salad-making, sandwich-making, soup-making, cake-baking, making nut roast or curries or pasta dishes or whatever for the evening menu, and then putting meals together when a check came on, the tab-grabber bristling with checks and all that information to hold in the mind and the timing to get right, the timing – that's what it was all about more than anything else. You had to work very fast, you had to be on the ball and it was quite stressful. Don't get me wrong, I mean it wasn't the hardest job in the world and it could be good fun too – working with the likes of waitress Taz (who was a friend of Sharon's) – but it just wasn't what I wanted to be doing at the time, which was *writing*. At the end of the shift I would go back to the flat, go for a run, and then get myself a meal and maybe have a couple of beers. I'd read a bit, but I'd have no energy for writing. And so, after about a month I left the job at the restaurant too and moved to the Purple House to 'live *my* life', which at that point mainly meant writing my novel.

in this real world

Why did I want to write a novel *anyway*? Well I suppose it all started at school – studying English and writing stories. The set texts, Shakespeare and Dickens etc., mostly left me cold, but the English teacher recommended that I read something extra-curricular, *The Catcher in the Rye* by JD Salinger, and this made a big impression on me. All my friends read it too and it became a big talking point among us. It was something we could actually *relate* to. After Salinger I read more American literature – Hemingway and Kerouac. And then, when I left school to go away to college, I read all kinds of stuff, but it was mainly American or French realistic novels that I liked. I wrote some short stories, poems and also some songs for the punk rock band that I was in. And I vaguely planned to write a novel, but at that stage in my life I didn't have the discipline or the life-experience to do it – though it remained a dormant aspiration throughout my twenties.

By my mid-twenties I was living in the Lakes and this coincided with my burgeoning creativity. The landscape and the lifestyle helped to draw it out of me. I did a little painting, but I preferred to write. I wrote some poems and I had ideas about writing a 'New Age novel'. I'd been reading a lot about green issues, alternative lifestyles and new age spirituality, and I wanted to write a book about turning away from the old established order and towards new, more enlightened ways of doing things. I'd stayed on a few communes too, which had inspired me. 'The old established order' was for me perfectly symbolised by 'the computer centre' – a government department where I had worked as a trainee programmer prior to starting my new life in the Lakes.

I wanted to write a novel because I felt the need to express myself. I felt the need to express myself, not just to *myself* but to others, to communicate my ideas and feelings to 'the world'. I always wanted to write about *ideas*, and my writing was always going to be basically *realistic*. Looking back I think my writing was probably *over*-concerned with ideas, and this first attempt at a novel, 'Communion', was little more than a clumsy vehicle for expressing my various ideas about the ills of society and the ideals that I aspired to. But as well as ideas there was a desire to write about the mundane things of daily life too – about relationships, and also the need to write *honestly* about my personal experiences in life. Jack Kerouac had a good definition of literature (as stated in *Satori in Paris*) as 'the tale that's told for companionship and to teach something religious, of religious reverence, about real life, in this real world which literature should (and here does) reflect.' When I was writing 'Communion' I was quite religious in my own way – and still am. But I hadn't yet broken free from traditional conservative notions of novel-writing. I hadn't quite broken free from the writing-by-numbers formula of the omniscient third person narrator, the need for a plot etc. – basically the crafted (and essentially dishonest) fictional tale/fantasy told at arm's length by an apparently god-like author. I hadn't yet found my own writing voice, and my writing wasn't yet really 'real'.

Anyway, I would become totally absorbed in my fictional world as I sat at my desk in the mornings and composed. I hated interruptions, such as when Mrs Vee would come knocking at my door to ask me to fetch a newspaper or something from town. I would tense up as I heard her laboured breathing as she walked slowly up the stairs. And then I would curse under my breath as she paused just outside my door to get her breath back. Finally she would rap on the door and I would wince as she called out 'Helloo, it's only me.' I would answer the door and try to be polite and try and get rid of her as soon as possible. The thing was not to let her into the room because once she was in I had a very hard job getting her out. She would ease herself down into one of the armchairs (where she would leave behind her distinctive odour), and she would prattle on about what she'd read in the newspaper or heard on the radio or seen on television. She was an avid newspaper-reader and Radio 4-listener and TV-watcher, and her head was full of all sorts of information about the sorry state of the nation. What she had to say was usually depressing and I usually switched off and just nodded my head and said 'hmm' now and again. Sometimes I would try and give her the hint that she wasn't welcome by saying 'oh really' in an off-hand sort of way, but she didn't seem to get the message that she was boring me and that I just wanted to be left alone. I wanted to be left alone to write about my saintly alter ego, to build my New Age castle in the air, and I didn't like having reality barge in on me.

When I finished the typescript after only four or five weeks I gave it to Sharon to read and make critical notes. She took it seriously and the notes she made were honest and helpful. Basically she was in tune with the spirit of the work, and she liked some of it, but on the whole she wasn't impressed. And pretty soon I wasn't impressed with it either. During the writing of it I believed in it, but once I'd got it completed I thought it was a failure. But there was *some* good stuff in there, stuff that could be developed – especially that opening section, narrated in the first person, about leaving the computer centre. It was only my first attempt, and I had a lot to learn. I'd read a few 'how to' books on novel-writing and I'd written 'Communion' in a fairly conventional style, mainly narrated in the third person with three main characters and a plot based around a woman leaving her husband (who represented the 'enemy') for another man (the 'hero'). But it lacked an authentic voice, it lacked credibility, and it lacked vitality. Also it was way too short to be properly called a 'novel'. Despite this, I got it photocopied and sent it off to a handful of publishers and agents before finally giving up on it.

skid row in the fells

In the midst of writing 'Communion' my dole money was stopped. It was because I'd left the tea shop of my own accord, and boss Chris hadn't played the game, as he had with Sharon – which is to say he told the truth that my job *wasn't* temporary. He was maybe sick of these people leaving 'to live their life', when he was stuck in the kitchen all the time. When I left and told him that it was to write my novel he was interested, and perhaps a little envious. He said something about how it would be good to take time out of the daily round, to stop the treadmill and reflect on life. He maybe thought I had some money, the cushion of 'savings' – which Sharon did, but I didn't. He'd gone back on his word to me, but it was forgivable.

I still had the part-time gardening job at the house in Keswick, and I managed to get a part-time job in a cafe in town too, although I got sacked from that after only a week. I'm not sure why I was sacked, but maybe it was something about my attitude, something to do with not taking their ridiculously zealous food hygiene rules seriously. Anyways, I was certainly struggling for money at this stage, and not paying rent to Mrs Vee. Sharon lent me some food money, and declared that she wanted to move into the house. I figured this would help me, as if she was paying rent it would take the pressure off me a bit.

So Sharon moved in and spent ages cleaning her room and making it her own. I don't know why she wanted to move in really because she had a much nicer place in town. Maybe her landlady had asked her to move out or something. Anyway, despite her best efforts to make Rigg Beck homely it was still a scruffy, dirty old place and a bit downmarket for someone like Sharon. She scrubbed at the stained bath to no avail, she brightened up her bedroom with colourful Indian cotton drapes, and she put candles in the kitchen – to Mrs Vee's consternation. (Apparently there had been a small fire in the house last season, when someone went to sleep with a candle burning – which set fire to the bedside table or something.) But despite Sharon's efforts, at the end of the day Rigg Beck was pretty much 'skid row' in the fells. (Someone had actually painted the words 'SKID ROW' on the bare floorboards in one of the top floor rooms, in amongst all the abandoned television sets, filthy mattresses and discarded random household objects.) And it was no place for a middle-class young lady, even if she had travelled round India and she was a bit of a hippy. I came back from my gardening job in town one evening and found her sitting at the old wooden table in the kitchen, eating her evening meal alone, with a candle burning for company – a 'table for one'. There were tears in her eyes and running down her cheeks, and it was such a sad sight and I felt sorry for her.

She didn't stay long in the house because after only a few weeks her parents came up from London to 'rescue' her and take her back home. Funnily enough a similar thing happened to a lad called Tariq, who had stayed at the house for a few weeks earlier in the summer. He was a bit hippified too, bummed around a bit, went to the jazz festival in town, drank beer with me down at the Swinny, and then was 'rescued' by his father, who drove him back down south where he was going to train to be a teacher.

Before Sharon left, Mrs Vee asked her to sign the visitors' book. She brought it up to the kitchen and left it on the table so that Sharon could do it at her leisure. When Mrs Vee went back down to the basement Sharon and I enjoyed reading through the book, seeing what people had written. It didn't go back as far as Ted Hughes; in fact it was only a couple of years' worth of entries I think, but a lot of people had passed through in that time, and most expressed gratitude for having experienced the unique ambience of the place. Some entries were a bit too gushing in Sharon's and my opinion. They were a bit sycophantic towards Mrs Vee. In my experience and in Sharon's too, Mrs Vee could be quite charming and interesting to a point, but she could also be very irritating, not knowing when to stop talking, and not knowing when she wasn't welcome to barge in on us. Or maybe she *did* know, and she did it anyway. But I don't think she realised how bad her body odour was. I think she very rarely took a bath, and she must have been incontinent. It's a shame, but no honest description of Mrs Vee could not mention this aspect of her, which some folk managed to turn a blind eye (or nostril) to, but which others found disgusting.

And another thing is that I don't think she realised quite how bad the condition of the house was. She'd been there nearly forty years and so I suppose the deterioration had been gradual and imperceptible to her. Also her eyesight wasn't very good. Anyway, I don't know when any maintenance work had last been done on the house but I think it had been a long time ago. A chap called Dennis, who came to stay for a couple of nights with his girlfriend Sheila, (they both having been tenants the previous year) pointed out to me that the woodwork at the bottom of the house was all rotten, and that one of these days the house was going to suddenly collapse on itself. This was not something that Mrs Vee would take seriously. As far as she was concerned a lick of purple paint was all that was required.

But going back to the sycophancy business, I feel compelled to say something regarding the myths that have grown up around Mrs Vee being some kind of philanthropic patron of artists and writers and actors. A lot of famous and not-so-famous artists and writers and actors have stayed here over the years, but they had to pay rent. (Or at least I *think* they did. Maybe some of the more favoured ones didn't.) She was only a landlady who appreciated the arts and who had been to art college and done some sculpting herself at one time. She wasn't a particularly magnanimous person, just someone who happened to own a big interesting house with enough space to let out rooms to help pay the bills. It was said that that she was descended from the Russian aristocracy, and also that she had connections with the Bloomsbury Group, but to be honest – so *what*? 'That don't impress me much', as the song goes. Why should it? I take people as I find them. It was an interesting place and you could rent a room cheaply because it was basic, it was spartan. Also there wouldn't have been much in the way of affordable short-term rented accommodation in Keswick when travelling actors such as Tom Courtenay, Bob Hoskins and Victoria Wood turned up to work at the Century Theatre in town (and probably none at all now). But, as far as I know she didn't take in people 'off the streets'. She was no charity. And the rent you had to pay for a room, although cheaper than what you'd pay in town, was not really a bargain when you considered what a state the place was in. Ah yes, the *rent*... By the time Sharon left the house things were getting a bit desperate for me. I'd managed to get a few more hours gardening at the house in town, which was enough to keep me in food and beer, but I still wasn't paying any rent, and in the end Mrs Vee asked me to leave.

the vagabond writer

In those days I used to cycle everywhere, as I didn't have a car. It was only four miles into town (mostly *down*hill into town). It was an old mountain bike that needed new brakes, and I had to remember that the brakes didn't work very well as I whizzed down the steep hill from Ellas Crag to Stair. At the bottom of the steep bit at Stair Mill the road bends sharply to the right, and straight ahead, just on the bend and propped against the stone wall, is a big old millstone with a chunk out of the edge of it – like someone had eaten a bit out of a 'Wagon Wheel' biscuit. One day I was hurtling down the hill and only just managed to take the bend. I had a vision of going over the handlebars and flying straight into that old millstone.

Some days I would cycle into town twice a day – maybe once for the gardening job, then again for food shopping or to go to the pub. Actually, if there was any pub-going it was usually to the Swinny, which was only about twenty-five minutes' walk, and therefore my 'local'. (At one time there had actually been a pub just a few yards down from Rigg Beck at Mill Dam – the site of an ancient corn mill. 'The Dog and Gun', later re-named 'The Sportsman' used to quench the thirsts of tourists travelling by horse-drawn coach on the journey back to Keswick from Buttermere, but it was demolished to make way for the Newlands Hotel, which eventually became the Purple House.) Anyway, to save money I'd been thinking about making my own homebrew, but since I was about to be evicted I wasn't in a good situation to make a start on that. Incidentally, I mentioned the phrase 'skid row' back there. When I check my dictionary for the meaning of this it says 'a part of town frequented by vagrants, alcoholics etc.' Well Rigg Beck wasn't in town, but it would be fair to say that I was a vagrant, and also someone with an alcoholic tendency. A vagrant is 'a person without a settled home or regular work' and I was definitely one of those. I could also, not incorrectly, be described as a 'vagabond' ('a wanderer or vagrant, especially an idle one'). The word 'alcoholic' is more difficult to define precisely as it is so relative, and perhaps the best definition is 'someone who drinks more than *you* do'. Anyways, I couldn't afford to be a proper alcoholic, and I only drank beer. But I was definitely a vagrant, a vagabond; also a writer, or *would-be* writer, but primarily a vagabond.

To get back to the cycling...I wanted to tell you that I used to cycle down to Ambleside once a month – mainly to get my hair cut at Johnny Williamson's. It was a long way to go for a haircut, but it was cheap, and it was an entertainment having your hair cut by old Johnny. He would put the world to rights as he worked the clippers on the number 2 setting, dressed in his white coat, and with a roll-up cigarette hanging out of his mouth, bits of ash occasionally falling and landing on your neck. He was always friendly – in his gruff, piss-taking Cumbrian way, and when the conversation started he always seemed to remember where I was up to in my wandering life.

Going to Ambleside was also an opportunity to visit the wonderful Fred Holdsworth's Bookshop. On one of my expeditions I bought a copy of Kerouac's *On the Road*, which Fred said was 'still selling well after all these years' I had read it before (a few times), but seemed to have lost my copy and wanted to re-read it. When I told him I was working on a novel he was interested. He told me that Melvyn Bragg had once been a regular customer, in his youth, and once brought in part of a manuscript of a novel for him to read.

responsibility of a writer

Anyway, I had to leave the Purple House, and thought about trying to find somewhere in Ambleside, but I ended up in the Duddon Valley – in what was pretty much the Duddon's equivalent of Rigg Beck – 'Browside'. I used to read the magazine *Resurgence*, and in the small ads at the back there was always this advert for cheap rooms to let in the Duddon Valley, 'sharing writer's remote farmhouse'. I phoned to enquire and spoke to the landlord, Peter Moorhouse. I arranged to go and have a look, and so one day I cycled all the way there via Ambleside, then over Wrynose and Hard Knott Passes, past Cockley Beck, then just a couple of miles down the road from there I turned up a rough track to the ancient-looking stone farmhouse.

Peter was a friendly old chap, in his sixties, a bit eccentric and alternative. He'd done various jobs in the past and had been married, but now he was on his own – except for the tenants and guests that stayed at the house. He showed me round the house and the room that was available – a decent-sized room (with a small desk) above the living room – and we agreed that I would move in. He cooked me a simple meal of omelette, potatoes and carrots, and offered me a glass of his home-brewed ale. Like me, Peter was a would-be novelist, and had his own Great Lakeland Novel on the go. He didn't have his own room in the house in order to maximise income from rent, and he slept in the attic. He used to stay up into the early hours every night, working on his book or reading, then emerge from the attic about lunchtime and potter about the house in just his Y-fronts, a grizzled, bearded old fellow with a piercing eye, and an eye for the ladies – of which there were usually one or two staying at the house. He was registered as a host with the Willing Workers On Organic Farms (WWOOF) organisation, although the place was hardly a farm. He had a few fruit trees, that was all, but he was in favour of organic growing and he liked the sort of people that it attracted – especially the female ones. I remember him going out for the day and on his return he asked if there'd been any phone calls. I told him that there'd been one from a 'Wwoofer', to which he said 'Male or female?' He was only interested in the female ones, who would come and stay for maybe a couple of weeks. They would have their own room and stay for free in return for some help in the garden. There wasn't actually much work to do in the garden at all – he just liked having them around for a bit of young female company. And they didn't usually mind that there wasn't much to do as they were intelligent independent types who were happy to spend time going off walking and exploring or staying in and reading.

There were also guests who came to stay in the summer for a week or two – simply for a holiday. And there were people like myself who came to stay, with the intention of staying over the autumn and winter months. I was hoping to progress with my writing. I hadn't entirely abandoned 'Communion', and had plans to break it down into a series of short stories. I had no intention of finding a job, not that there were any jobs going in that part of the world, especially now that it was the 'back end' of the season. I managed to claim Unemployment Benefit, though I had to cycle an undulating sixteen miles to Millom to sign on. I was able to claim Housing Benefit too. The rent was quite low and the council paid it all – directly to Peter. It looked like I was going to be nicely set up for the winter, with a room to write, fells on the doorstep, a genial landlord and a steady throughput of interesting visitors. But despite the initial promise, I found that I couldn't get on with the place, and in the end I only stayed for a few weeks.

During my time there I did a fair amount of reading, if not writing. I read short stories by DH Lawrence and Kafka, *Cockley Beck* by John Pepper (a chapter of which describes a 'merry neet' at Browside with Peter and others), and various articles in old *Resurgence* magazines that were stacked in the living room. I came across an article by Rosalind Brackenberry and

John Mitchell called 'The Responsibility of a Writer', in which John Mitchell said: 'A writer's first responsibility is to himself, to purify his own mentality; for if the source is polluted, all that flows from it is tainted also.' This struck a chord with me. I felt the purification process should be about throwing off conditioned ideas about writing, ideas that were learned at school or college and from all the 'how to' books written by 'experts'. The only way to proceed with my writing was intuitively, on my own terms, drawing inspiration from writers whose works I appreciated as a reader, and making *honesty* the number one ideal and bedrock of what I wrote. I wanted to strip away contrivance, falseness, politeness, 'fiction' from my work. I wasn't interested in pandering to some conservative bourgeois validation of my work (and the activity of 'literature', and the 'judging' of literature in this country is very much dominated by a deeply conservative middle class). I wanted to write honestly about my own experiences. And yet I was still trying to write fiction, to fictionalise my experience in the set of short stories drawn from 'Communion'.

But I didn't get much writing done at Browside. It was too noisy. My room was above the living room and there was no noise insulation in that eighteenth century farmhouse. Voices rose up and I might as well have been in the same room. I put my ear plugs in at night and they muffled the noise a bit, but I was still kept awake. I seemed to be alone in my desire to go to bed early and get up early in the morning. There were two women staying, on holiday from Ireland, and they stayed up late every night, chattering on and smoking in the room down below. The cigarette smoke irritated me too. What had been so promising turned out to be no good at all. I would go out fell-running during the day – up Harter Fell, or onto the Coniston fells, and then come back to a room full of people chattering and smoking and playing opera records on Peter's old gramophone. The place was in the middle of nowhere, but there was no peace to be had there. I had wanted solitude, but it was denied. I felt trapped. All I had was the fells and, to be honest, they weren't turning me on much at that stage. The Duddon Valley is very pretty and relatively unspoilt, but for me it lacked the sublime beauty of Newlands or Buttermere. It was so big and wide open, with the fells quite set back. There were interesting twists and turns, and some nice bits of woodland. It was pleasant, pastoral, peaceful, but lacking in drama, excitement, inspiration. And I began thinking that maybe I had overdone the solitude thing and that I had to get back to 'the world', back to 'The Great Street of Life'. I needed more social life and stimulation. And I began thinking of going back to university.

I first went to university in Lancaster after school, to do a Geography degree, but dropped out after the first year. I couldn't concentrate or take it seriously. It was partly the sheer relief of leaving home and finding a life of relative freedom, but mainly that I couldn't see the point in absorbing a lot of factual information that seemed to have nothing to do with my life and that wasn't taking me anywhere I really wanted to be going. Where I *did* want to be going I didn't really know. I vaguely dreamed about working for the youth hostels in the Lakes, but I thought I wouldn't have the required skills. I did plenty of non-curricular reading and I started writing stories and writing songs for the band, of which I was the singer. But after a term I stopped attending lectures and seminars and I stopped writing essays. I simply couldn't see the point of doing the degree course anymore.

But the idea of going back to university still held some appeal for me. I wasn't bothered about getting a degree, but I was interested in the intellectual stimulation and challenge that it offered; also I was attracted to the social opportunities. And so, towards the end of August, I suddenly made the decision to go back to college. I managed to get a last minute place through 'clearing' on a Literature and Philosophy degree course at Bolton Institute of Higher Education. It all happened very quickly, but my stay at Browside was over and I moved down to Bolton, the town of my birth, initially staying with my grandmother until I found a room in a shared student house. It seemed like a good idea, but things didn't work out and I only stayed for one term at Bolton. There was only one module on the course that really interested me – about writers and the evolution of society. I didn't really make much effort to make friends there either. I was restless and I wanted to commit myself more fully to my writing 'mission'. Also I was in the wrong place. After living in the Lake District, living in Bolton was too much of a shock to the system and I hated it. I'd felt trapped at Browside, but here I felt *really* trapped. Urban living was a nightmare for me – the sheer volume of people and traffic, the noise and ugliness and lack of open space. In my desperation I managed to buy a cheap second-hand car out of my student loan so that I could drive out of town up the A666 to Belmont and go running up Winter Hill. This gave me some respite, but for most of the time I couldn't relax. I changed my accommodation a few times, but it was just a case of 'out of the frying pan into the fire', and in the end I gave up and moved back to the Lakes. I sold the car and rented a room in Ambleside.

a kindred spirit

The shared house in Ambleside was another noisy place and I started thinking that I should try and go back to living at Rigg Beck in order to find the peace and quiet to get on with my writing. The place was calling to me. Funnily enough I bumped into Mrs Vee in Ambleside library and when I asked her if I could move back she said 'maybe', but then when I phoned her a week or two later she said 'no'. And so I carried on living in Ambleside, making very little progress with my writing, but throwing myself into running. I also got a job at a veggie cafe in Grasmere. I pulled away from the writing and moved increasingly to running – which was easier and healthier. Perhaps I needed a rest from the writing, and running kept me sane and grounded in the world. At the same time I hadn't entirely given up on my writing mission and had vague ideas about living in a tent up in the fells to save money, and writing in the public library – or even in the tent. I saw myself as possibly sitting cross-legged in a small dome tent and typing away at my old portable typewriter. But these mad ideas gave way to the more sensible and realistic scenario of going to work in a kitchen at the veggie cafe, living in a shared house, and doing loads of running.

At the end of the season I moved to the quiet hamlet of High Wray, near Hawkshead, where I lodged with a friend. And here I found the peace and quiet I needed to still the mind and eventually return to my writing. I also got a job at the bookshop in Hawkshead, which helped me to discover some inspirational reading. Among other things I read Bukowski, Camus, various New Age stuff, and Henry Miller's *Tropic of Cancer* and *Tropic of Capricorn*. I was hugely impressed by Henry Miller's work; this was a major discovery and inspiration for me. There were passages and sometimes large tracts of 'The Tropics' that dragged, that seemed like self-indulgent verbal diarrhoea. But there were other passages that were like gold and, all in all, these books were inspiring. What was it about Henry Miller? I think *honesty* more than anything else, and an indomitable human spirit, a *vital* spirit. He was honest about himself and honest about the world he lived in. He seemed to have broken free from social conditioning to a large extent, and he was his own man, independent and clear-thinking. He was also very sociable and interested in other people and had a great generosity of spirit. His writing was a generous gift, and in reading his books he came across to me as a friend, a kindred spirit. Like Kerouac, he inspired me and showed me what was possible.

After a season at the bookshop I ended up working as a waiter at a pub in Hawkshead. I hated the job and I was desperate to leave and concentrate on my writing. I was determined, nay *compelled* to have another crack at the novel. This time I wanted it to be a 'completely' honest confessional-autobiographical novel. It was something I had to do, whatever the cost. But it was impossible whilst I was in full-time employment at the pub, which drained my energy and my creativity. I needed time. I needed to *immerse* myself in the project. And so, after the busy Christmas period I jacked in my job at the pub and set about writing 'Only Human'.

I wish I had 'Only Human' and 'Communion' to refer to now, but alas I threw them both away several years ago. All that work, all that hope consigned to a wheelie bin and a landfill site. A4 ring binders containing neat typescripts (that never made it onto computer files). So I have to go from memory, and from my journals – which, thankfully, I have kept. 'Only Human' was basically the story of my leaving the computer centre to go and live in the Lakes, getting a job at the veggie restaurant and a room at Rigg Beck, and trying to write The Great Novel. There was still some fictional element, but it was essentially an autobiographical novel and a definite development from 'Communion'.

I managed to claim dole and work pretty much full-time on writing 'Only Human' over January,

February, March, and part of April '96, composing by hand and then typing it up on an ancient second-hand electric typewriter that I'd recently bought from Steve at the bookshop in Ambleside. When I finally finished typing up the final draft in early April I was completely skint, with various debts and a few weeks behind with my rent. I had to get a job. As luck would have it, I received a tax refund of about five hundred quid – which came at just the right time. I paid off my debts and still had enough to buy a second-hand burgundy-coloured Mk1 VW Golf. I had a celebratory day out in Keswick, where I caught up with some old friends. I also visited the tea shop, only to discover that Nigel – who had been a waiter the last time I worked there – was now the owner and boss. Taz was still there working as a waitress; also a girl I knew called Sarah was now working there as a waitress too. They were all very friendly, and I asked about getting a job there. Nigel said that he would need help in the kitchen from about mid-May. And I kept thinking that I had to move back to Keswick, get a room there, and return to work at the tea shop. I'd forgotten how many people I knew in Keswick, and it felt almost like a homecoming.

And so I went back to work in the kitchen at the tea shop, initially commuting from High Wray, and then moving up to Keswick to rent a small room in a shared house on Main Street. And it felt like I was returning to The Great Street of Life, after a lonely hermitic novel-writing winter in the 'hideaway cottage' in High Wray. And it seemed like my life was starting to imitate my art, my writing. The new cook, Pat, said he used to be a computer programmer and that he was renting a room at Rigg Beck. And part-time chef Donna – who was my landlady at Main Street – reminded me a bit of Sharon.

When I moved into the house on Main Street Donna was away on holiday with her young children. I had the place to myself for a couple of weeks, but when they returned I realised that the house was going to be far too noisy for me. It was only a cheap rent for a very small room but I couldn't relax in the house at all once Donna and the kids were there. The kids had a room next to mine and they made a lot of noise – shouting and running around. I was out during the day, working day shifts at the cafe, but as soon as I walked through the door when I got home in the evening I felt paralysed by the noise. It was certainly no 'room to write', and I had to look at alternatives. I bought a tent and thought about camping, I looked into renting a flat in Cockermouth – which was too expensive, and finally came home to the idea of moving back to Rigg Beck. I phoned Mrs Vee and she said 'Yes'.

PART TWO

a beautiful morning

So here I am, back at Rigg Beck. Why didn't I come here sooner? It's so quiet and peaceful here, and right in the fells – surely a great place for a fellrunner and a writer to live! And Pat is good company – a kindred spirit in some ways it seems. He's been reading 'Only Human' and talking about it and giving me useful feedback. He says that it's an 'honest' book, and I think it is, and yet it does contain some fiction and this fictional process seems to be a way of distancing myself from experience, a way almost of being dishonest. Perhaps I could be more honest and write a better book if I were to write more or less straight autobiography mixed with reflections on writing, life etc.

The time now is 7.30am and I need to set off on my bike into town to go and work at the tea shop. I get my stuff together, and it's another beautiful summer's morning as I open the big old front door and wheel my bike out of the hallway into the strong sunlight. And then I'm pedalling and freewheeling down that road, turning off right at Ellas Crag, down into Stair (taking care to slow down for the hairpin bend with the millstone dead ahead), over the bridge past the Newlands Adventure Centre on the right, then up the hill to the Swinny, then down again, through the woods, past the entrance to Lingholm Gardens, into Portinscale, over the suspension bridge and into town.

Town is waking up to another day. The shops are mostly not open yet, but people are on the move, on their way to work or making an early start for a walk. I cycle up Main Street, past the Moot Hall, down Borrowdale Road, then down Lake Road to the tea shop. I wheel my bike round the back and unlock the door into the kitchen. The clock on the wall, which is a bit fast, reads 8 o'clock. On the stainless steel work surface there is a slip of paper on which is written: '4 full, 2 veggie, 1 beans on toast'. I fire up the oven and change into my white jacket and blue and white checked trousers – the breakfast chef. I select what I need from the fridge and put the sausages in the oven. Then I go into the dining room to check that the places are laid and sort out the cereal and milk and fruit juices etcetera. Two of the guests, an American couple, let themselves in through the front door and tell me that they've had a stroll down to the lake. 'What a beautiful morning it is!' she exclaims enthusiastically. And it *is* a beautiful morning.

I get the breakfasts cooked and start serving from 8.30am. We say that breakfasts are served between 8.30am and 9am (or earlier by special arrangement) but everyone has turned up at 8.30 this morning – which makes my job easier. There are three couples, and one chap on his own. The place gets a mixture of punters, but quite a few are attracted to its 'green' credentials. Ten per cent of the profits are supposedly donated to causes such as Greenpeace, BTCV, Animal Aid etc., and the place is listed in various green and vegetarian directories. When the owner set it up it was vegetarian, but it's not been veggie since Nigel took it over.

After waiting on with the breakfasts I have a good look in the fridges to see what we've got and see what I need to make for the day shift. I also check the temperatures in the fridges and freezer, and see that one of the fridges is still running too hot. I'll remind Nigel about that later. As far as food goes, there isn't a lot to make – just some scones and a load of mixed salad. (There's loads of soup left from yesterday.) I start with the scones, using a vegan recipe I picked up from the veggie cafe in Grasmere. Instead of using milk it uses orange juice, which helps them to rise and also gives them a nice golden colour.

At 9am Sarah and Scott arrive. Sarah will clean the dining room, take payment from guests, clean the guests' rooms, and then wait on tables over lunchtime and the afternoon. She's a pleasant girl, usually smiling, unless Nigel has upset her – which he often does. She's a wiry-built outdoorsy type, ex-YHA, bespectacled, very intelligent and probably too intelligent to be here, but then so are so many people in the Lakes – graduates many of them, doing menial jobs. She's good for a conversation and a laugh is Sarah, but she can be a bit ponderous, a bit lacking in confidence in her work – which might be what annoys Nigel. I can be a bit lacking in confidence myself as I too am an 'amateur' here. I've not been to catering college or got any cooking qualifications. I've learned on the job in youth hostels and cafes, and I'm okay, I can do the job, although when it gets very busy I'm not as fast as some. I sometimes feel that I'm blagging it, that I'm not *really* a chef, but I have to pretend to be professional. But who is really *anything* in this world of jobs? You can train for a particular job, go to college and get bits of paper to prove that you are the real thing, which will give you confidence that you are who you say you are, but it doesn't necessarily prove much, and if it becomes your only identity and function in society then that is a sad state of affairs – although that *is* the state of affairs for the vast majority of people in this world that we live in.

Scott is the 'kitchen porter', which means he will do the washing up, and help me where necessary. He's a young local lad, a bit unstable, but good at his job when he puts his mind to it, and good for a crack in the kitchen too. He's had a troubled background, been in trouble with the law a few times, and even done a stint in a 'youth custody centre', but he's got a broad smile, he's hard-working and the boss likes him. He walks through the back door, a tall slim figure in jeans, trainers, t-shirt and baseball cap. He says 'Morning!' removes his cap, runs his fingers through his crew-cut hair, then says 'I got shitfaced last night', and laughs. He gets 'shitfaced' quite a lot does our Scott, often with chef Paul, who will be in later for the evening shift. They both drink a lot and also smoke a lot of dope. I look up from my scone mixing bowl and say 'Morning Scott', and see that his eyes look bleary. 'How art thou?' he says. 'Not so bad,' I say, and in fact I do feel quite good today – calm, at peace. The sun is shining and there isn't much prep to do and it shouldn't be too busy today. It's mid-June and so it's not quite high season yet. The schools haven't broken up yet, and it's fairly quiet on weekdays. Scott puts his cap back on, collects up the dirty breakfast plates, rinses them off, then places them in the ancient dishwasher that doesn't work very well.

Sarah comes into the doorway to watch me rolling out the scone mix, and cutting out the round shapes. There isn't much for her to do until the guests depart. She's wiped the tables clean, and now she has to hoover the floor. 'Would you like a coffee?' she says. 'Yes, I would Sarah, thank you,' and so she pours one from the glass jug on the coffee machine. The breakfasters didn't drink very much and there's plenty left. She puts the white mug down carefully on the worktop, next to the unbaked scones. 'How is the Purple House?' she says. 'I want to come and visit you some time.' 'Yeah, good, come up after work one evening.' Then she gets going with the hoovering, a compact wiry figure that makes me think 'rock climber', though in fact she is more of a walker and a swimmer.

I get the scones baked and a big bowl of mixed salad chopped (lettuce, cucumber, tomatoes, mixed peppers, red onions). We have the radio on in the kitchen – Radio One, and the tunes help to pass the time, and help us to work. At the moment it's *Don't Look Back In Anger* by Oasis. Scott and I both like this one and we sing along to it. He soon has the washing up done and he goes out the back for a smoke. The back door looks onto the car park and it's also a popular route taken by locals coming and going. He shouts over to a friend – 'Hey Shaun!' A lad of his own age sidles over in his baggy tracksuit bottoms and lights a fag and they talk for a bit and laugh about whatever it is they did last night. 'Can you get me some more of that stuff?' says Scott.

Lunchtime comes round, Sarah has finished cleaning the rooms and we're ready for the lunchtime trade. Nigel pops in briefly, takes some money out the till and announces that he's off to play crazy golf with his friend Mike. Fair enough, we're not likely to be busy and we don't need him. Also we can relax more without him. Customers trickle in and we sell a few soups and sandwiches and salads, and also a couple of omelettes – which I have put on the 'specials' blackboard. Omelettes are quite easy to cook to order and the customers can have what ingredients they like. I'm serving them with new potatoes and salad. Personally I think an omelette should always have *cheese* in it, and onion and peppers are good too. We don't have many frying pans, but as long as we don't get more than two ordered at the same time we'll be okay. We've got a couple of these really heavy cast-iron frying pans that are great for doing omelettes.

It gets to about two o' clock and our lunchers have gone. I decide to have an omelette for lunch myself, and so does Sarah, and we sit at a table together in the dining room. Scott makes himself a ham sandwich and comes to join us. And it's nice to have a leisurely sit-down lunch on the job like this – which is unusual. The music playing in the dining room is a classical CD, Vivaldi's 'Four Seasons' or some other such ubiquitous tea shop musak. Scott turns his nose up at it. 'This is the sort of music that *dead* people listen to' he says – which makes us laugh. 'But we *are* dead, aren't we?' says Sarah, and we all laugh again. And we *are* dead in a sense, I suppose. I mean this is hardly what you'd call 'living'. We all want to be somewhere else – like out in the sun, doing something else, but for the time being we are stuck in this tea shop, slaving away for three pounds-fifty an hour. Okay, so we're not exactly working hard just now, but you know what I mean. I don't care much for the classical music either, and Sarah isn't bothered either way, so we turn it off. Now we can hear *Killing Me Softly* by The Fugees coming from the radio in the kitchen.

We sit there for a while, and then some people come in. It's Anna from Windsor House, with her new housemate Lila. They want tea and cake. Scott disappears back to the kitchen and Sarah gets them their tea and cake. I stay at the table and Anna and Lila sit down to join me. Anna is a regular patron of the tea shop, and an adopted daughter of my former landlady at the flat in Keswick, where I lived before I lived at Rigg Beck the first time round. She's dark-skinned and I think she may be of South American origin, although she's got a completely English voice. She also has a deformed hand and people say she has some kind of serious health problem, though I don't know what it is. Anyway, she's a friendly and cheerful person and she introduces me to Lila, who moved into Windsor House a few days ago. Lila is a girl of about sixteen, slim, with long fair hair, a few freckles, innocent blue eyes and a gentle manner. She says that she's new in town, having just finished school and moved over from a town in the North-East – Sunderland, in fact. She has a soft Geordie accent. 'I want to get to know people,' she says. 'I want someone to take me out for a drink.' I take a look at her pretty face, then say '*I'll* take you out.' She smiles demurely. 'What are you doing after work?' she says. 'Come over to the house for a cup of tea, if you like.'

quickly and naturally

Windsor House is just around the corner from the tea shop. I lived there myself once – for a few months in the winter of '93 – before I moved to the flat on the outskirts of town, the flat in Anna's mother's house. And I have good memories of my time there. I had a good large room at the back of the house on the first floor, and with a good view out towards the Derwent Fells. The landlord was a jovial old chap called Jim, and the room I had was actually his daughter's, but he let it out whilst she was away travelling. It was in this room that I planned out my book 'Communion', before writing it at Rigg Beck. The rent was quite cheap, and it was in fact one of the few shared houses in Keswick where you could rent a room cheaply. I remember Sharon coming round once, and she described it as 'the hippy house', and there was an element of that about it. There were people who lived there who had previously lived at Rigg Beck.

Anyway, here I am now knocking on the front door, visiting young Lila. The handle turns, the door swings open and there she is, smiling at me, dressed in a white tee-shirt and a flimsy white cotton skirt. 'Come in,' she says, and I follow her down the corridor to the kitchen at the end, observing the movement of her buttocks under the thin material of that skirt. She puts the kettle on and we sit down at the table, upon which stands a freshly-baked carrot cake – baked by her own fair hands. 'Would you like a piece, Sol?' 'Yes, that would be nice.' And so we drink tea and I eat some of her cake (which is very nice) and she asks me what it's like working at the tea shop and tells me that she's working part-time on the checkouts at the supermarket but 'it's boring and I'm looking for something else, more hours, preferably in catering. I wouldn't mind working somewhere like the tea shop.' 'Well, you never know...people come and go.'

'Do you want to see my room?' she says, which of course I do. So she leads me just a short way back down the corridor because her room is here on the ground floor, at the back of the house. It's a fairly large room with a double bed, a big wardrobe, chest of drawers, a couple of chairs and a desk by the net-curtained window – overlooking a small car park. There are lots of girlie adornments – some pictures of horses and a boy band pin-up and a bright pink cuddly toy sitting on one of the pillows on the bed. 'Take a seat,' she says and so I sit on one of the two chairs. 'Would you like to see some photos?' And she gets an album and pulls the other chair next to mine and she turns the pages and shows me some pictures of her house back home – an ordinary-looking council house, her elder sister, and their pet dog – a fierce-looking Alsatian. I wonder why she left home, but decide it might be a bit indelicate to ask. She leans in towards me as she points out a photo of her best friend, Tracy, and her face is only inches from mine. She seems so young, so gentle and open with me. I sense something in the air between us, and as I move closer to look at the photo and put my arm around her it just feels natural and inevitable. She melts into me and the sides of our faces touch. She bends to put down the photo album and then turns to face me and we kiss - just a little awkwardly at first, but then a long delicious snog. She tastes sweet. I run my fingers through her long fair hair. My right hand holds her head and my left hand goes under her tee-shirt to feel the bare flesh of her midriff. I hear her breathing get heavier. We pull away, smile at each other and then kiss again, but it's a bit awkward in these chairs and so I suggest we move over to the bed. She nods and gets straight up and walks the few steps to the bed, my gaze entranced by the movement of her backside. She kicks off her flip-flops and lies down on the bed. I take off my trainers and lie down beside her, on my side and propped on one elbow, admiring her young body. Her bare feet, with red-painted nails, and the pale skin of her slim legs – revealed up to her knees - is enticing, and I want to see more. I move over her and lie on top of her and we kiss again, more passionately this time. As my hands move under her tee-shirt to her breasts, and under the skirt up to her thighs, she makes appreciative little 'mmm' noises. I reach around her back, unhook her bra and push up the tee-shirt to reveal her small pointy white tits. I take them in my hands and suck on the hard pink nipples, and she reaches down and fumbles with my fly, and before too long I'm screwing her under the inscrutable gaze of that cuddly toy.

We both come, and lie there in peace for what seems like a long time. I realise that I hadn't thought about wearing a condom. It all happened so quickly and naturally that I didn't think. But she says 'It's okay, I'm on the pill.' And I'm amazed at how quickly it happened. I only met her for the first time a few hours ago, and now...the sexual energy, the chemistry was there and it happened. And why not? I tell her that I'm a writer and am trying to get a novel published. She says she's a writer too and has had stories published in women's magazines. 'That's amazing,' I say 'for one so young'. And she *is* young, just sixteen I think, and I feel perhaps I shouldn't have said 'for one so young' – drawing attention to our age difference, for I am 33 and old enough to be her father. But it doesn't matter because she obviously fancies me, and she says that she needs 'a steady mature man'. Well I may be relatively mature in years, but I don't know if I could accurately be described as 'steady'. Perhaps I am steady relative to her, I don't know. I don't know her, though doubtless I will be *getting* to know her.

provided providentially

Cycling back up the Newlands Valley in the mellow evening sun I'm feeling quite pleased with myself, naturally enough. I feel like I need to make sense of this encounter with Lila, but then *why* do I need to think about it? It happened and it was good, and it will probably happen again. And it's been a long time since I had a lover, a girlfriend, so I should just enjoy it and be grateful for that which has been 'provided' for me, provided 'providentially'.

Back at the house I sit on the bench on the verandah for ten minutes and drink a can of *Stella*. And then I go in and have a bath, and as I get undressed I can smell Lila's natural perfume on me – which excites me a little. And then after my bath I make a simple meal of pasta with mushrooms and beans, then sit in one of the armchairs in my room and listen to some music – the recently-released album by Electronic, *Raise the Pressure*. The cover has a representation of an angelic-looking child kneeling on the ground and plucking daisies from the grass under a blue sky with fluffy white clouds. The music is upbeat electro-pop, wistful songs of love and romance - and it seems to fit my mood.

Finally I go to bed – which is actually a mattress on the floor rather than a proper bed. I can hear the sound of running water in the beck, and an owl hooting in the trees. And then I hear the sound of a car pulling up outside the front of the house, and the front door banging shut. It'll be my housemate Pat, back from his evening shift at the tea shop. He comes up the stairs to go to the bathroom and then goes back down to his ground floor room, the Blue Room, where he'll probably relax by smoking some weed and listening to music with his headphones on. He's quite considerate, and I don't see much of him with me working the day shifts and him working evenings. As I'm nodding off to sleep I hear the sound of a mouse scurrying across the floorboards.

play the game

I said to Lila that I was a writer, but a writer is someone who writes, and I haven't done much for a while, though I do have plans for a project called 'Suicide Notes', which I have started. It's a monologue by someone who, because they are about to do themselves in, can be completely honest about themselves and society etc. (though when I think about it I don't see why being suicidal should be a prerequisite for that). Anyway, I haven't been able to get beyond the first couple of paragraphs, so it doesn't seem to be going anywhere. I've moved on from it now really, or rather I *should* have moved on from it. But it still has some kind of hold over me. I'm not suicidal myself but I am interested in how the suicidal impulse can relate to honesty, and I am interested in writing ever more honestly.

Talking of suicide, I recently called at a designer clothes shop in town where an ex-girlfriend of mine works. She was depressed about having no money and about the whole deal of having to work forty-odd hours a week for very little pay. She's living in Cockermouth because she can't afford to live in Keswick, which means she has to run a car, which is a big expense, and she can barely afford to live. I sympathised with her. It's pretty much the same for me, and the same for so many people. The gap between the rich and the poor is ever-increasing. You play the game by going to work full-time in some job that you don't really want to be doing, just to survive, to pay the bills, but it isn't enough and you end up getting into debt with nothing even to show for it. When she first moved to the Lakes and we started seeing each other we both worked for the youth hostels, which was a relatively cushy number. The downside was living in, but we had more free time and more disposable income. But now this is 'the real world' of working in a shop (or kitchen) and renting a room in a shared house and commuting and of living in a country, in a society, in an area where it isn't enough to work forty hours a week – not unless you have some sort of private income, or a highly-paid partner or you are living with your parents or something. It's difficult to see how a town like Keswick will be able to function in the future, with its complete lack of affordable housing and all its 'service sector' jobs that just pay the minimum wage. It seems that half the people that work in the shops and kitchens of the town commute from West Cumbria. Anyway, what I wanted to say was that she said she would commit suicide in a couple of years' time if things didn't improve. It was the sort of thing I might say myself. It's sad that people should end up thinking like this, just because of the socio-economic situation, but that is the bottom line: *the socio-economic situation.* It's all very well living in a beautiful area and doing the outdoorsy thing and having friends etc., but if the wage from your full-time job isn't enough to meet your basic living expenses then living itself is not a realistic option anymore.

naked and vulnerable

Another person that works in the clothes shop is Wayne. He's a friendly South African guy, in his early-forties with a craggy weather-beaten face and piercing blue eyes – and he's a writer. He invited me round to his flat one evening, where he fed me pizza and salad with white wine, and showed me some of his own writing. He doesn't actually have a typewriter and it was all handwritten in his illegible scrawl – so he read some passages out to me. It was all quite personal stuff about the break-up of a relationship he once had – though rendered in a traditional third person narrative. He's been writing for years and is very well-read, but I found it strange that he'd never bothered to get himself a typewriter. Although he claimed that he hoped to get his work published I got the feeling that he was only really writing for himself – as a means of coming to terms with this broken relationship. He talked confidently about literature and writing, and he talked too much, but when it came to sharing his own writing with me his confidence dropped. Anyway, he was interested in seeing my writing, and so I left him a copy of 'Only Human' to read.

He returned it to me a couple of weeks later, with some notes that he'd made. His critical skills are quite sharp, and you can tell that he's studied literature at university. Some of his feedback I agreed with, such as that the 'book' was too short, and that some of the fictional material at the end wasn't believable. But the one point that stood out for me more than any other was that he said that it was 'not fictionalised enough', that it was 'too personal'. This seemed to misunderstand what I was trying to do because what I actually wanted to write was 'personal' stuff, and the weak points in the book were where I had *overly* fictionalised. If I was going to develop as a writer I had to move *away from* fiction.

Since all literature is in its essence self-expression, the more openly and frankly confessional the writing the better. Exposing to the reader what I really feel and think is more important than 'art'. Self-disguise through fictionalisation comes down to cowardice, even if it does conform to the widely-accepted impersonality doctrine. As Henry Miller put it in *Big Sur and the Oranges of Hieronymus Bosch*: 'The writer who wants to communicate with his fellow man, and thereby establish communion with him, has only to speak with sincerity and directness. He has not to think about literary standards – he will make them up as he goes along...he has only to deliver himself, naked and vulnerable.'

A writer may be 'one who writes', but it's necessary sometimes to take time out from writing and just get on with living. I've spent the winter writing 'Only Human', but now it's the summer I want to feel more human by going out to work and socialising and running on the fells and seeing Lila. Unto everything a season, and perhaps now is 'a time to dance'. Not only do I need to take stock of what writing I've done, and what writing I am going to do next, but also – given that I have set out my stall as an *autobiographical* writer – I need to do some more living to accumulate some material!

this is the life

It's a beautiful sunny day, a day off from the tea shop, and I'm running beside the beck, the steep bracken-covered slope of Causey Pike rising up on my right. After a couple of hundred yards the path takes me past the house water supply 'reservoir' – a square tank sunk in the ground and covered over by some stone slabs. The tank is fed by a small stream that runs off Causey. I pause to remove a slab to look inside – and I see that the water level is fairly low. We're having quite a hot dry summer so far. I replace the slab and resume my run, trotting along steadily, heading into the hills, disappearing into the wilderness. After a while the path starts to climb, gradually getting steeper, but I keep on running and I'm feeling comfortable. Up on my right, on the steep fellside, is a patch of stunted ancient oak trees. Hundreds of years ago they would have covered the fells round here, but now there is just this small remnant, together with another patch on the other side of Ard Crags at Keskadale. Ard Crags is the name of the ridge rising up on my left, above Rigg Screes. The path keeps rising and the terrain gets stonier, until the gradient finally levels out at a grassy pass. The pass isn't named on the Ordnance Survey maps but I call it 'Rigg Hause'. On one side flows Rigg Beck and on the other flows Sail Beck – so it could equally be called 'Sail Hause'. From here I often strike up the steep grassy slope of Ard Crags and then turn left at the crest of the ridge to return, over Aikin Knott, back to the house – for a relatively short evening run. But today I've got plenty of time and I'm going to go further. I'm going to go up the other side – up the steep heathery slope onto the ridge called Sail. From there I'm going to run the route of the Buttermere Sailbeck Race – in reverse (and missing out Causey Pike, which I have already by-passed), which means going up onto Crag Hill, then to Whiteless Pike, down to Buttermere village, then up the Newlands road a bit and then along a faint path above the beck, then up the steep nose of Knott Rigg, along the ridge to Ard Crags, and back down to the house from there.

The climb up through the heather is very hard work. There is no path and the higher I go the steeper it gets. The heather is deep and springy and strength-sapping but I manage to keep going at a walk, lifting my legs high and grasping at the heather with my hands, pulling myself up – such that I am pretty much on all fours. If I'd had any sense I would have tried to locate the path heading the other way towards Scar Crags and gained the ridge that way, but I like a challenge and I like a direct route. It's a hot day and I'm not wearing any top. I feel more at one with Nature like this, like a wild fell animal just doing my own thing and with as little between my skin and the skin of the fell as possible. The noon sun beats down on my bare back and I'm sweating as all four limbs, heart and lungs are working hard to propel me steadily upwards. Finally I make the ridge and my legs feel jellified, but once I start trotting along through the rocks they feel okay. Next it's the scramble up through the crags onto Crag Hill, which is the highest point on my route. I pause at the trig point to take in the view of Hopegill Head and Grasmoor, and then begin the fast grassy descent down to Wandope Moss and along Whiteless Edge to Whiteless Pike. From Whiteless Pike it's a steep fast and exhilarating descent to Buttermere. I pause briefly to take in the fantastic view of the High Stile ridge on the other side of the valley and then check the time on my watch: 12.15pm. I wear a cheap Casio digital watch, which is good for running as it has a stopwatch facility. I press a button on the side to bring up the stopwatch screen, press another to zeroise the reading, then another to set it going. The tenths-of-a-second digits start changing at incredible speed, and then one, two, three seconds...and I throw myself off the top of Whiteless, pretending to myself that this is a race, looking for all the best lines, the most direct, the fastest route. I've descended off here many times before so I know what I'm doing, although I can't remember every twist and turn of the ground and there are always choices to be made, split second choices about where to put my feet in order to get from the top to the bottom in the fastest possible time. There are some crags to negotiate, some corners to cut, and I take most of this first steep drop away from the path (which is getting quite eroded nowadays). Down, down, running and jumping over the grass and rock, completely focussed, one-pointed, intense, a glorious madness, fast feet dancing, fast mind anticipating the ground just ahead, the split-second decision to veer to the right or the left, down to the grassy flattish bit, then the narrow contouring path, then the sudden veering off to the left through thick grass and bracken to cut the corner and rejoin the path, then suddenly leaving the path again, dropping straight down the very steep slope to the junction with the Rannerdale Knotts path, some walkers here stopped and watching me - some crazy person in a big hurry, rushing past them and bounding down the smooth-clipped fell turf on a super-fast green path through the bracken, down, down through a gate and to a house on the left and a rocky outcrop by the road. And I reach for my watch and press the stop button and look at the digits - 10:02. Ten minutes and two seconds – that's not bad, not bad at all. I swing my bum bag round to the front, unzip it and take out a small water bottle. I have a drink – and the water is warm from my body heat and the heat of the sun. And then I jump off the rock onto the road and jog down through the village – where there are quite a few cars and people walking around, some of them with ice-creams. Past the Bridge Hotel on the right, then up the road past the tiny church on the left, then left at the junction and up the tarmac for a hundred yards, my legs struggling a bit after that breakneck descent, then veer off the road onto a faint path – little more than a trod that runs below the road and parallel to it, above the beck that is here named 'Mill Beck' on the map, but which becomes 'Sail

Beck' further upstream. And then I cross a small stream and it's up the steep nose of Knott Rigg, and after an initial jog I slow to a hands-on-knees style of walking, striding up the grassy ridge, and it's another hard climb and my heart and lungs are having to work hard again but my body is rising to the challenge, I've got the bit between my teeth, and I'm moving well, I'm in control. I went through a tired section back there, but now I've re-found the mad energy that wants to push my body onwards. The sun is beating down out of a clear blue sky and I'm feeling the heat but I'm also feeling good. This is the life, this is living. And I'm pushing hard up the fell, sweating, and I'm feeling strong and vital and virile. I glance up at the sun and my vision is momentarily blinded. I pause for a moment and put my hand on my chest and feel my heart's rhythmic pumping. I swing my bum bag round and have a swig of water, then carry on, striding hard up the slope. And when I get to the top I break immediately into a run – and this is a great ridge for running, from Knott Rigg to Ard Crags, a couple of ups and downs but mainly quite level running, the ridge narrowing to an edge at Ard Crags, with views down to Rigg Hause on the left and Keskadale on the right. I push on, down the narrow path through the heather of Aikin Knott, scampering down the rocky bit at the end, then bounding down the smooth grass, veering off to the left near the bottom of the ridge to cross the stream Rigg Beck, then down the path to the road and Rigg Beck, the house. I sit on the bench on the verandah for a bit, recovering, then take off my shoes and go into the house for a bath and a bite to eat (bread and cheese and a bit of salad stuff). And then I set off into town in the car.

the market place

The burgundy Mk1 Golf looks good parked outside the front, and Mrs Vee approves of the colour – which goes with the colour of the house. Incidentally the colour of the house is not a uniform purple but at least two shades, the front of the house currently being a light shade – almost lilac, and the sides being a darker shade. Also the gable end at the front is in the darker shade. Mrs Vee told me that a group of gypsies last painted the house, and stayed at the house whilst they did it. They didn't do a particularly professional job, but then Mrs Vee probably didn't pay them much for doing it. Who cares anyway? It's the Purple House, not the Swiss Lodore Hotel. As long as it stays purple, that's all that matters. (Nowadays nobody would be allowed to paint their house purple in this National

Park, but because it was painted purple before the planning regulations came into force it was allowed to stay purple - a Lake District oddity.)

Anyway, I drive down the valley into Keswick, where I want to do a bit of food shopping and look round the outdoor shops and then visit Lila later. It's pretty busy in town but I can park in one of the allocated spaces in the car park at the back of Windsor House. Lila is working at the supermarket, but she'll be finished at four o'clock and so I'll meet her at the house soon after that. I walk through to the Market Place and quite enjoy watching all the people, mainly visitors, milling around. There is for me a sort of romance about this town, and the Market Place is at the heart of it. There are all the outdoor shops, the pubs and cafes, and the Moot Hall – which is nowadays the Tourist Information Centre. On Saturdays there is an open air market, and then the place is 'gay thrang', but today is a weekday and so I suppose it's just medium-busy. I head up Station Street to an outdoor shop called 'The Call of the Wild'. I look at a Lonely Planet travel guide to New Zealand and dream of travelling there. And then I look at the clothing, and in particular a *Patagonia* fleece that I've had my eye on for a while. It's a pullover style in a dark green and it fits me well but it's very expensive – but then it is very good quality, being *Patagonia*.

I've been spending too much on outdoor gear since I moved up to Keswick. I've just got myself a credit card but I don't want to be getting myself into big debt over stuff I don't need. Then again my clothes are old and wearing out and I could do with a decent fleece. Of all the things I think I need it's the fleece more than anything else that I want to buy. It seems to have some kind of symbolic or talismanic significance for me, beyond its practical value. I've tried on quite a lot of different ones in different shops, but this one is the best. I am anxious about it because I am used to living hand-to-mouth with no spare money for such things and – if I were more sensible perhaps – I would save my money for when I need it for more essential things such as rent or food or car repairs. But this credit facility is somehow 'burning a hole in my pocket', as they say, and so I finally decide to buy the fleece. I pay with my card and feel sheepish, almost guilty about doing it, but I am after all an outdoorsy-type and the jacket will doubtless be very useful. It's just that it's the most expensive one of its kind. I suppose I've got expensive tastes, even though I do live at the Big Wreck and I'm just a cook in a tea shop. I walk back down Station Street with the jacket in the plastic carrier bag with the shop logo on it, and I feel like just another consumer, a materialistic punter kitting himself out from the outdoor shops (which are pretty much half the economy of this town, the other half being 'hospitality' and catering). I take it to the car and put it in the boot.

Next I go to the supermarket, which is called *Caterite,* and which is where Lila works. Here I buy a few staple food items and some cans of lager. I wonder if I should get some bits and pieces to eat with Lila later, but she said she wants to make some kind of meal for me. I look out for her and see her at a till with a massive load of shopping on the conveyer belt. We exchange a little wave and then I buy my bits and bobs at one of the baskets-only checkouts. And then I walk back to the car with my two carrier bags, which I deposit in the boot, and when I look at my watch I see that Lila will be home from work in only twenty minutes. I decide to go into St. John's churchyard and just sit on a bench and admire the view out over Derwentwater to the Derwent Fells, some of which I was running on earlier. I'm feeling physically relaxed after that run – not tired, but actually *vivified*. I feel strong, centred, calm, lucid. And I'm looking forward to making love to Lila.

too much information?

I sit in the churchyard long enough to give her a chance to get changed and sort herself out before going round to see her. And I find the waiting hard and realise that I'm impatient to see her. When it gets to 4.30pm I get up from the bench and walk the short way to Windsor House. I ring the bell, and when she comes to the door she looks great with her hair down and a grin on her face and she's dressed in that thin white cotton skirt again, and with a white blouse thing knotted at the front to reveal her lean pale belly with a pierced navel. We have a quick kiss and then she asks me 'Have you had a good day?' I say 'Yes, I have' – which I have. 'And *you*?' 'Not really,' she says, and pulls a face, 'But you're here now,' and she grins again. She leads me down the corridor and I can't take my eyes off the movement of her backside – which jiggles just a little as she walks, and I realise that under that almost see-through skirt she isn't wearing any knickers. As soon as we're into her room and I close the door I take her in my arms and we have a long delicious snog. My hands move down to her arse and she makes an appreciative 'Mmm'. And then I lift that flimsy skirt at the back and feel her bare buttocks and she smiles and closes her eyes and says 'That's nice.' My hands move round to her front and I can see that she isn't wearing a bra either, her already-erect nipples poking at the thin cotton fabric. I unbutton the blouse so that it falls open to reveal her perfect pointed little teenaged tits. I take them in my hands and suck on first one, then the other. Her breathing gets heavier. And then we move hand-in-hand over to the bed. I sit down on the edge of the bed to take off my shoes, and she kneels on the carpet in front of me, her hands snaking under my tee-shirt then taking hold of it at the sides and pulling it upwards. I take it off and she strokes and kisses my chest, her hands gradually moving downwards until she's stroking my ever-hardening cock through the fabric of my jeans. She unzips them and her hand goes in and she strokes me through my briefs. Then she undoes the button and pulls on the waistband. I raise myself off the bed and she pulls both jeans and briefs down below my knees to reveal my cock pointing rudely at her. I sit down on the bed again and she grasps it, takes it in her mouth and sucks on it greedily, making appreciative 'Mmm' noises. Then she looks up at me and says 'I'm feeling *so* horny.' It's because I'm coming on, and I'm a complete nympho at this time of the month.' 'I'm feeling pretty horny myself,' I say as I pull her up by her armpits and remove my jeans. She takes off her blouse and skirt and lies naked on the bed. And I lie over her and we kiss, and then I move down her body, kissing her tits, kissing her belly, kissing the insides of her thighs, and finally moving down below her thick pubic thatch to kiss her perfect fresh little flower of a cunt. I prise open her lips and taste her sweet pearly nectar. She moans and writhes around a bit as I pleasure her, and then I move up to kiss her on the mouth. 'Let me go on top,' she says, and so I lie on my back and she pulls on my cock then straddles me and puts it inside her and rides me with a wet clicking noise as she moves up and down. 'Oh god that's good,' she says. I hold her thighs and watch her tits jiggling and her face, with eyes closed and mouth half-open, as she moves up and down over me. And in the corner of my eye I see a tabby cat in the corner of the room, watching us. 'There's a cat!' I say. 'I know,' she says, 'I'll tell you later. And then I pull her off and lay her down on her back because I want to do her this way. And it doesn't make any difference to her she says, and so we do it 'missionary', which is better for me and I can fuck her harder this way and she loves it and she's making soft little moans and she's getting close as she runs her sharp fingernails up and down my back, and I'm close now too, and as her face twists and she cries out I let myself go, my cock pulsing with what feels like a huge load of come. (Dear reader, is that 'too much information'? Would you rather not hear about such things, such elemental stuff of life? Perhaps in reading this book you were hoping to learn a lot of historical facts about the Purple House, and perhaps this sexual material is not to your taste? Perhaps you would rather stay on the surface, perhaps you would prefer it if these private things were merely alluded to rather than described openly and honestly. But, hopefully, you are not that kind of reader and you are someone who actually appreciates a writer who will reveal himself and his life as openly, nakedly and unashamedly as possible. And it goes without question that sex is a vital part of life.)

We lie entwined for a good while, relaxed and breathing in the scent of sweat and sex, and also a stale unpleasant smell – which I realise is to do with the cat. I can see a litter tray in the corner of the room. 'What's with the cat then?' I say. 'Oh, it's a stray that I rescued,' she says. 'Don't you think you should let it out?' Maybe open a window so that it can come and go.' And I realise that this room is stuffy, with the windows closed on a warm sunny day. And the odour from the litter tray is not pleasant. The cat, as if it knows it's being talked about, sidles up to the edge of the bed and miaows plaintively. 'But it might not come back,' she says. 'But you need some fresh air in here!' I open the top half of the sash window and a light breeze wafts the net curtain. We get dressed and I suggest we go for a walk down to the lake and take the cat with us.

So we go outside and the cat trots after us, then suddenly bolts across the road to the house on the other side, where there's a well-dressed middle-aged woman sitting in the small garden. The woman sees the cat and calls to it 'Tibby, where have you *been*?' She looks over to us, sees Lila and says to her 'Did you steal my cat?' Lila is lost for words for a moment. 'I thought he was a stray,' she says, and then to me

'Come on,' and she takes me by the hand and leads me away, down Lake Road. She tells me that she phoned Animal Rescue and that she's innocent and I believe her, but it's a bit weird. Anyway we forget about it, and as we walk past the tea shop we wave at Taz, who is standing near the window with no customers to wait on as yet. It's a bit early in the evening and a lot of people are strolling around, enjoying the evening sunshine. And Lila and I stroll down the road, under the underpass – where there is a busker strumming on a guitar and singing the Oasis song *Wonderwall*. On we go, past the crazy golf course, past the Blue Box Theatre and into Crow Park, where we sit down on the grass. She's wearing that flimsy cotton skirt (with knickers on this time) and the blouse and she looks very attractive, but also very young – young enough to be my daughter, and I feel that all these other people walking around must surely notice this and be thinking what a dirty old man I am, or maybe just a *lucky* man, I don't know. Anyway I don't feel at ease with her in public. She kisses me and calls me 'my darling', but it doesn't feel right. I mean I hardly know her. She tells me that she hates her job at the supermarket and asks me about the tea shop. I tell her what it's like and she's interested. I know she wants a job there. But there isn't much else to talk about. I tell her about my fell run and she listens patiently but I feel she has difficulty relating to it. It's like we're on a different wavelength really. Anyway, after a while we walk back to the house, where we eat a meal of quiche and salad stuff that she got from the salad bar at the supermarket. She's a vegetarian, like me – so at least that's something we have in common. Then we go to bed again for another fuck, but it isn't as good this time. And then we go out for another walk and go to a nearby pub, 'The Four in Hand', where I enjoy a couple of pints. She doesn't drink much and she's too young to be drinking in pubs really anyway, but she keeps me company with a half of lager. Again I feel conscious of the age difference, and conscious that we're not conversing much.

Finally we go back to the house and go to bed to sleep, except that I can't sleep beside her because she keeps fidgeting and moving around. Every time I manage to drop off she wakes me up as she shifts position in the bed. I sigh and ask her to please be still, but she can't help it she says, and perhaps she can't. After an hour or more of this I decide enough's enough. I'm very tired and I hate having my sleep disturbed and I can see I'm not going to get any sleep in bed with Lila so I say to her that I'm sorry but I'm not going to stay the night after all, and she apologises but understands and lets me go without too much fuss. And so I drive back to Rigg Beck at half past midnight, feeling exhausted and disappointed that the day should end like this.

essence of the life-force

Lila and I have started this relationship – if you could call it that – but we're not really a couple, not really 'going out' with each other. I don't really love her, and to me she's just a mistress. I don't want a proper relationship with her because of the age difference and because we have so little in common. We don't connect at all on an intellectual level, or pretty much on any level except the sexual. I think she wants more from me, she wants a proper relationship, but I just want no-strings sex or a 'convenience fuck', as I think of it. And this is how it's been for the last couple of weeks, and she patiently goes along with it, letting me have her on my own terms. But I feel bad about it, bad about 'using' her (although whether or not I'm using her any more than she's using me I really don't know).

Anyway, I don't want to hurt her feelings and I keep thinking I should finish with her before things go any further. In fact I *did* finish with her the other day. I said I just wanted to be friends. But then the very next day I went round to see her and we ended up in bed. She only has to offer up her body and I can't say no. And, to be honest, I don't really have a good enough reason *not* to keep seeing her. She isn't exactly 'right' for me, but then she isn't exactly 'wrong' either. Anyways, fucking Lila has become part of my daily routine. I generally go round to her place after finishing the day shift at the tea shop at five 'o clock. We have sex, but then afterwards we don't have much to say and so before long I cycle back to Rigg Beck, maybe go for a run, have a bath and a meal, read a bit, drink some beer, listen to music, and maybe chat to Pat, if he's around.

Pat has already cut his hours at the job because he isn't enjoying it and he told me he probably isn't going to stay much longer. He doesn't have any previous experience in catering and he's finding it too hard. He finds it very tiring, and he complains especially about his tired legs. It makes me wonder what he's been doing all his life, though I think he said that he'd been on the dole for three years in Liverpool before moving up here and he simply isn't used to work of any kind, let alone physical work. It annoys me that he's only paying £15 a week rent for his room, whereas I'm paying £30. Admittedly his room is smaller than mine and not as good, but it's quite a big difference in money. And Mrs Vee told me that he was trying to negotiate paying even less. She said that he 'pulled a fast one' when he first came to enquire about a room and 'I hadn't got anybody in'. 'Pulled a fast one'- that sounds like Pat. He seems like such a nice bloke, but he is a bit of a con man, and he's very tight with his money. He hardly buys any food, eating mainly at the tea shop, and he's stolen food from the tea shop to bring back here. He's earning plenty of money but he acts like he's got none and he's got this policy of not spending. On the other hand he is quite good company and he's okay for a conversation. He's a handsome bloke with his long shiny black hair and a sun tan and a smile and a glint in his eye that catches the attention of the ladies - and I can see how he would have charmed and conned Mrs Vee. But although he enjoys female company he's more interested in practising his yoga and staying celibate. I talked to him about my 'relationship' with Lila and he said that he would never get involved with anyone on that basis, that it was either a full-on serious relationship or nothing for him. He told me that he masturbated every day, and he thought that was better than getting sexually involved with someone who wasn't 'right'. Well I could see his point, but for me I think it's better to be fucking Lila than to be jerking myself off on my own in my room. It's better to have someone than no-one. It's saying 'yes' to life, it's living in the here and now, it's making the most of that which comes my way rather than turning up my nose and holding out for something better that might never actually materialise. Scott at the tea shop said to me 'You can do better than that', but what is 'better'? Why should I presume that I am too good for Lila? I don't think I am. In fact I think that in some ways she is too good for me. We're not a good match, that's all. But we *are* sexually attracted to each other and the sex is...how can I put it? The sex is vivifying, vitalising, life-affirming, *living*.

I remember how Sharon used to talk about sexual energy being the essence of the life-force and how as sexual beings we are instruments of this life-force. She said that sexual energy is the divine energy that animates the universe. Repressed sexuality drains our vital energies, weakening all our mental and physical faculties, but fulfilled it becomes a great creative and regenerative force. And I believe that it *is* a regenerative force, and that my own life-force or spiritual energy has become stronger since I've been seeing Lila.

check on!

It's a Friday evening and I have to work at the tea shop because Paul, the usual evening chef, hasn't turned in and Pat couldn't work as he's gone home to Liverpool for the weekend. Paul has given a week's notice of quitting the job as he's got himself a job cheffing at another restaurant just a few doors away. Whether we'll actually see him again at work here now I don't know. He's mates with Scott but Scott doesn't know, or at least won't say, what Paul is up to. And so I've been thrown in at the deep end of doing an evening shift on a busy Friday night, after having worked the day shift too. Actually it was pretty quiet during the day, and it was quite a good crack with Sarah and Scott. Nigel said I could knock off at four o' clock this afternoon to give me a reasonable break before coming back to work. I went round to Lila's, from where I went for a quick run up Walla Crag and back, followed by a shower, a salad meal prepared by Lila, then back to work at the tea shop for 5.30pm. There was no time for a fuck. Scott is still on a break but he'll be back at 6pm. He usually works both day and evening shifts and clocks up a huge number of hours per week. He generally takes a break between four and six o'clock. The tea shop doesn't close at all between shifts and we sometimes get people coming in for afternoon teas up until six o'clock, but at six the tea shop becomes a restaurant.

I get changed into a clean set of kitchen whites and clear the pile of dirty plates and cups and saucers from the stainless steel work top. There's a backlog of washing up to do for Scott, but he'll soon get it shifted. I checked the fridges earlier to see what we need and I did some prep this afternoon – some boiled new potatoes, tagliatelle pasta, brown rice, and a load of mixed salad. I also made a chick pea chilli – which is my own vegetarian input to the evening menu. I'm pleased to say it's been going quite well, although vegetarian punters seem to be in the minority here now – unfortunately – and I'll have to do quite a lot of meat meals this evening, and maybe even some steaks.

At six o'clock Scott arrives and dives straight into the washing up. As well as being the kitchen porter he will also be my commis chef this evening. I am the acting *head* chef – which is a bit scary, and I hope I'll be able to cope. Also at six the waitresses Taz and Emma arrive, and Nigel pops in briefly to make sure we're all here, then disappears again. Taz was working here the previous time I was here – in '93. She's a very attractive girl with long dark hair, big brown eyes and a broad smile. She comes from Leeds, but she's been living in Keswick for a few years now. She did a stint living at Rigg Beck, and she left the tea shop to go travelling to India, then came back and is now living with her boyfriend Tom. She's also now a trained aromatherapist and she does a bit of that during the day and is hoping to get enough work so that she doesn't have to work here as a waitress, but for the time being she's still working here a few nights a week. Emma is a bit younger and she's at university down in Exeter, where she's doing an English Literature degree, and she's just back home in Keswick and working here for the summer. I've only met her briefly once before, but I wouldn't mind getting to know her better. She's got long fair hair and a sweet intelligent face. She's also an ardent born-again Christian – which ought to put me off, but doesn't. That last time I saw her it was around changeover time at the tea shop and a guy called Matt, who also waits on here some evenings, was giving me some tapes he'd made from some of his CDs. He has a big music collection and he likes to share his musical tastes and I thought it was quite generous of him to do the taping for me. Emma said she thought it was immoral to do 'home taping', and at first I thought she was joking, but she was dead serious and she said she would never do it herself. I thought it was a bit of a mad puritan stance to take, but I still fancied her and thought I'd ask her out for a drink some time.

Anyways I'd better put my mind to the job because a couple of punters have come in and they've made their order and here comes the lovely Taz now with the check. She hands it to me and I take a look: 2 x goat's cheese starters followed by 1 x chick pea chilli and 1 x chicken curry. Okay, that's easy enough. I start on the starters by slicing off two discs from the goat's cheese log, placing them on a couple of pre-prepared crostini and putting them under the grill. And whilst the cheese is warming through and browning just a little on top I arrange some piles of mixed salad leaves in the centre of two large white plates. Once the cheese discs are done, so that they are just melting a bit over the crostini, I remove them and place them on top of the salad leaves. Next I place a couple of slices of oily roasted red pepper over the top of each cheese disc – such that they look like pouting wet lips, then finally I liberally drizzle the whole thing with the thick jism of vinaigrette, some of which (as per Nigel's instructions) I spatter 'artistically' around the edge of the plate. Then I ring the little brass bell and Taz appears in the kitchen again, all smiling. 'Ooh, they look good,' she says. And then she whisks them away to the salivating punters, or 'mangers' – as a chef I once worked with calls them. That was at the pub in Hawkshead where I worked as a waiter. He used to tell me to go into the bar and ask people 'Will sir and madam be *manging* this evening?' Anyways these two early birds with the goat's cheese are our only customers so far and there isn't much for Taz and Emma to do. Emma comes into the kitchen, dressed in a smart blouse and skirt and asks me if I want anything to drink. 'You're all right Emma,' I say, 'I'll just have tap water.' 'I'll have a pint of *Becks*!' calls Scott from the dishwasher in the corner. It's a bit early for boozing on the job and he's only joking, but he often does help himself to bottles of *Becks* on the evening shift (when Nigel isn't around). 'So, Emma,' I say, 'How's it going at uni? Are you enjoying the course? What books are you studying?' 'Oh fine, yeah. We've been doing Victorian novelists this last term – the Brontes, George Eliot, Dickens...' 'And what sort of stuff do you like to read?' 'One of my favourite writers is Jane Austen. Have you read any of her work?' 'No, I can't say I have. I've never felt *drawn* to it, to be honest. Have you read any Jack Kerouac?' 'Never heard of him,' she says. 'What about Henry Miller?' She shakes her head, and I'm thinking to myself – that's typical, the universities are stuck in the past, stuck in the *Victorian* era with their ultra-conservative canon that won't admit anything interesting or vital that's happened in the last fifty years, nay *hundred* years. Why go to university to study English if you are *really* interested in literature, in writing? Why study English Literature at university at all? What can it be good for except for producing more English teachers and lecturers to perpetuate the whole irrelevant system? Oh yeah, and of course as a middle-class rite of passage for middle-class young people such as Emma. It's something they can put on their CV, something that proves they can write an essay, that they can absorb a lot of prescribed factual information and then regurgitate it in the prescribed manner. And it will help them to go on to do some other (usually completely different) course, thereby delaying actually going out to do a job of work in the real world. Well, good luck to 'em I suppose. If they've got rich parents to support them in their meaningless endeavours, then why not? Personally I think the best reason to go to university is to get away from home to meet new people and have a few beers and a few laughs. Anyway, where was I? Emma is looking at me, waiting for me to say something perhaps. So I say 'What kind of music do you like, then?' 'Oh all sorts...George Michael.' Okay, I can see this isn't going anywhere. We have completely different tastes, outlooks and backgrounds, and she's completely flat-chested too, and yet I still can't help but fancy her. Maybe it's the *challenge*. Maybe I'll convert her to my way of thinking. 'Emma!' calls Taz from the dining room. Quite a few *mangers* have just come in and Emma needs to do some work As she walks back into the dining room I watch her backside move under the skirt. It's fairly large, but sexy. All that sitting at desks writing essays about *Wuthering Heights* or whatever, and not enough exercise. And just because her backside is sexy doesn't mean to say that she actually *is* sexy. She could be frigid, and judging by her taste in literature she probably is.

Anyways, anyways, it's time for me to do some work now too because here comes Taz with a check, followed closely by Emma with another. 'Check on!' says Taz as she slides the slip of paper into the tab-grabber, and 'It's a steak' says Emma as she slides her slip in next to Taz's. A steak! Damn! But it was inevitable... Apparently this restaurant used to be a steak place years ago, and it seems to be going back that way, despite the fact that it's still listed in the vegetarian guides. Right I'm going to have to focus on what I need to do now. That first check has a soup and a hot pink grapefruit starter, followed by a pork in cider casserole and a creamy mushroom tagliatelle. The second one has no starters and it's a chick pea chilli and a medium rare beef steak with boiled potatoes and veg of the day (carrots and broccoli). And I'd better get the mains going for that first check – a chick pea chilli and a chicken curry – which means microwaving the cooked rice and heating portions of the chilli and the curry in small saucepans on the hob. I'd better get that steak out of the fridge and under the grill soon too, though I don't want to overdo it as they've specified medium-rare. I don't like having to do steaks, and in fact this is the first one I've had to cook for years. I am a vegetarian, after all. I don't like handling the stuff and I don't like the smell of it cooking, and I know that the degree to which a steak is cooked is a common cause of customer complaint in restaurants. I know what 'medium-rare' means, but will that correspond to the customer's idea of what it means? The soup needs heating up and likewise the pork casserole and mushroom tag, and the grapefruit needs to go under the grill – before the steak. (We definitely don't want any steak juices on the grapefruit), and it's all systems go now with various things to juggle, such that the timing is right and things are hot and ready to go out at the right time, in the right order. One thing I have learned in this game is that being a good chef is more about being quick and well-organised than it is about being a particularly good cook. Scott asks me if I need a hand. I wonder whether to delegate the steak to him, but decide I'd better do it myself, so instead I suggest he does the mushroom tag and pork in cider. There's no rush, as they've got to have their starters first.

And so the evening goes on, and more checks come on, and Scott and I work well as a team and everything goes smoothly and everything is co-ordinated and there are no complaints. I do find it challenging, quite a bit more so than the day shift, and it is a bit stressful, but also satisfying to get things right. And at the end of the evening, with the last of the meals cooked and the washing up done Scott and I decide to go for a pint at The Cellar Bar. There are actually still two punters in the dining room, lingering over their desserts and coffee, but Taz will look after them and then lock up. Emma has already gone home.

At The Cellar Bar, which seems to be the town centre pub favoured by the locals, Scott and I get a pint – and we're both drinking the *Bitburger* lager that they serve here. I actually enjoy real ale, but after a shift in a hot kitchen on a summer's evening I reckon the *Bitburger* is more thirst-quenching and I have to say it hits the spot nicely. Also in the bar is Paul, our absentee chef. We see him as soon as we walk in, propping up the bar on his own, also drinking the *Bitburger*, smoking a roll-up and apparently half-pissed. I ask him where he's been – to which he says 'I've been here, man' (in his Geordie accent). 'But what about your job at the tea shop?' 'Aw man, I've left. I'm not working for that wanker Nigel no more,' and then he breaks into a laugh, which turns into a coughing fit. Scott laughs too, and I can't help but smile, though I am a bit pissed-off that he dropped me in it – into doing the evening shift *he* should've done. Oh well, I get paid by the hour and it's all extra money (and we got about a fiver each in tips tonight too – something that you don't get on the day shift). Scott lights up and I can see that he and Paul want to catch up so I down my pint pretty quickly and don't hang around for long. They are talking about some dope that Paul has scored and Paul says to me 'We're going to get wasted tonight!' Both he and Scott are wearing these cannabis leaf pendant things round their necks, like it's a badge of their religion or something – the religion of getting wasted on weed. 'Have a good night lads. See you tomorrow Scott.' And I leave them to it and walk back to my car, which is parked at the back of the tea shop. Taz is just locking up as I pull out into the car park. There are some lights on in the upstairs rooms, and there are a few guests staying. There is no member of staff staying overnight on the premises, which probably isn't as it should be, but if there's an emergency the guests can ring Nigel's number, and he doesn't live too far away. Paul lived in the small attic room for a while, and I thought about doing it myself before I moved to Rigg Beck, but there's no privacy and you end up being constantly on call. Anyway I drive off, back up the road to Newlands, back home to Rigg Beck. It's too late now to be visiting Lila. I'm knackered, and I just want to have a quick bath and then go to bed.

winning me over

It's another beautiful summer's morning as I'm cycling into town to do the day shift at the tea shop. I'm a bit tired from last night, but I'm feeling positive and this four mile bike ride is invigorating and will set me up for the day nicely. It certainly is a beautiful commute, and what some people wouldn't give for this... It beats driving on the motorway, that's for sure. I especially like the section beyond the Swinny, which is nearly all downhill, the road twisting and turning through the trees, and then at the turning for Nichol End you go round a bend and there is an amazing view of Skiddaw, which looks absolutely massive from here – a great big majestic grey mountain. Then it's into Portinscale and over the suspension footbridge over the River Derwent. Sometimes I have to dismount and walk over here if there's some early morning dog-walkers or fellwalkers coming the other way, but usually there's nobody around at this time of day and I can pedal across. There's nobody this morning so straight over I go, then it's through a gate on the other side and through the fields to come out at Greta Bridge and the Italian restaurant. I turn right here onto Main Street, past the Co-op on the left and Donna's house on the right. And there's Scott walking along the pavement, just past Donna's, walking in bare feet and looking a bit dazed, a bit out of it. I shout over to him 'Hey Scott!', and he raises his arm half-heartedly, and I'm not even sure he recognises me.

At the tea shop I unlock the back door and get the key to the boiler room, which is a sort of annexe at the back here, and where I've started keeping my bike. The boiler room is also where we keep all the 'chefs' whites' – the thick double-breasted white cotton jackets and the blue and white checked trousers which we have to wear. Some firm supplies them and launders them and we're supposed to have a set of three or four each. Anyway, they're kept in here and this is where we get changed. There's also a washing machine and a tumble drier in here, which is used for laundering the guests' bedding and towels. And I sometimes use it for my personal laundry, since there is no washing machine at Rigg Beck.

Right then, into the kitchen, which is as we left it last night, except for a couple of dessert plates and coffee cups. Taz has left me a note for the breakfasts: 4 x full and 4 x veggie. That's easy enough, and I get on with cooking them and then serving them when the guests come down at 8.30. And at 9am Sarah arrives, as usual, but not Scott. Oh well, he'll probably turn up soon. Sarah makes us both a coffee and then she gets on with her jobs and I get on with mine. I have to make some soup today, some scones, some salad stuff, and some more chick pea chilli. The soup will be celery, as we've got loads of that in the back store, and I do like celery myself. I get on with that first, and I love the smell of it cooking, sautéed in olive oil with onions and garlic and plenty of black pepper in a thick-bottomed saucepan, sweating it off for a bit before I pour in some hot water straight from the kettle – so that it boils like mad at first and the kitchen fills with steam and the strong smell of celery and onions and garlic. I switch on the extractor fans and now people in the car park and the Fiat garage (next door) will be able to appreciate the savoury smell too. I leave the pan to simmer away for a while and get on with the scones. And once my scones are in the oven I add some veg stock to the soup and then blend it with the huge stainless steel stick blender. Next it's the chick pea chilli. It's not a hot chilli and in fact the dominant spices are coriander and cumin. The recipe I got this idea from called it 'Spiced Indian Chick Peas' but 'Chick Pea Chilli' runs off the tongue better and Nigel reckons it looks better on the menu as it's an instantly recognisable concept for the punters. I chop up a load of onions, mixed bell peppers – red, green and yellow, and some garlic, and sauté this lot in a pan. I add dried cumin, coriander, paprika and cayenne chilli pepper and keep the pan on a high heat, stirring the veg and spice mixture so that it doesn't stick. Then I open an A10 tin of chopped tomatoes and pour this in and then leave the mixture to simmer away for a while. Then I add an A10 tin of cooked chick peas and stir them in. Finally I add some melted coconut block, to thicken it up and give a bit of body and a bit of sweetness. And once that's done I leave it on the back of the stove to cool down and get on with the mixed salad.

At 10am Donna arrives. She only works here very part-time now (although she used to do a bit more when Nigel took the business over and she helped him set up the menus). She's an experienced chef and used to work for *Club 18-30* holidays. She's from West Yorkshire but for some reason she ended up in Keswick and now she's a single mum with two young kids – those two young kids that I decided I couldn't live with. Anyway she breezes in through the back door, and in her loud voice announces to me 'I shagged Scott last night!' then beams a broad expectant smile at me, one eyebrow cocked. There's a pause, then I say 'Well done!' and she bursts into laughter, a mad cackle that ends in a rasping smoker's cough. I'm glad she didn't shag *me*, and I remember how when I was lodging with her for that brief period there was one evening when she was reclining on the sofa with a glass of wine, the kids gone to bed, and she offered me a glass and she had something in her eye that seemed to be giving me the come-on but I didn't want to know. 'Where's Scott?' I say. 'I dunno, is he not *here*?'

Anyways, she gets on with making some soda bread and a tarte tatin and a couple of quiches whilst I finish off my chick pea chilli and then chop up some salad. She asks me how things are going with Lila and gives me a wink, but there's not much I want to say about that and I don't really like people knowing that I'm seeing her. I guess Scott must have told her. She tells me a bit about the places she used to go to in the Mediterranean when she worked for *Club 18-30*, and she obviously misses it and wishes she were young again and leading that kind of lifestyle. Maybe last night's drunken liaison with Scott reminds her of it. She says she's got a bad hangover and she won't hang around for long. And once the quiches, the soda bread and the tarte tatin are in the oven she asks me to keep an eye on them and then scoots off at about 12 noon.

Ten minutes later Scott rolls up and apologises for being over two hours late and says he got shitfaced again last night and now his head feels 'cabbaged'. 'I hear you had a good time with Donna,' I say. He shakes his head, runs his hand through his hair, then finally laughs. 'I'd better get on with the washing up,' he says. 'Yes indeed,' and there is quite an accumulation now – all the breakfast crockery and pots and pans and all the stuff that Donna and I have used this morning. 'Aw...I hope I feel better later,' he says. 'I didn't get any sleep last night...I feel like shit.' 'You'll be reet after a couple of hours of this,' – and I hope he will because I'm relying on him to help me and it's a long afternoon and evening ahead. 'Oh, by the way,' he says, 'Lila's been sacked from the supermarket – for nicking stuff. Someone told me in the pub last night.' 'Oh really,' I'm not entirely surprised because someone else told me recently that she'd been caught stealing from a market stall a few weeks ago. It does worry me though, obviously.

It's 12.30pm now and punters are rolling in for lunch. Nigel arrives and tells me that he's already got a replacement chef for Paul – a guy called John who will actually be starting this evening. Well that's a relief for me. Nigel wants me to come back this evening and just spend an hour or two with John to make sure he's okay and then, assuming he is, I can scoot off. Happy days. It gets quite busy over the lunchtime period with soups and sandwiches and salads and jacket potatoes and quiches (though *not* omelettes, which I've scrubbed off the specials board). Today's specials are quiche and salad for the veggies, and ham salad for the carnivores. Nigel helps Sarah out the front over the busy period, then at two 'o clock he's about to leave when who should appear at the back door but Lila. She asks him for a job, 'Whatever hours you've got, part-time will do.' He says 'Can you bake cakes?' She says 'Yeah, I can' then he goes 'Well, you can start now and bake a couple of cakes, a carrot cake and some other cake.' Her face lights up. He takes her round to the boiler room to show her where the uniforms are kept and she comes back dressed in an oversized jacket and trousers, with her hair tied back, and looking quite cute. I show her where the ingredients and the recipe books are and she says she doesn't need recipes and gets cracking on the carrot cake, cracking eggs into a large plastic bowl. 'How's it going at the supermarket?' I ask her. 'Oh, I've left. I couldn't stand it anymore.' She's got what she wants now – a job at the tea shop. It's a bit weird for me, her being in the kitchen, a colleague, but I don't know how many hours Nigel will give her. I suspect not many. She'll maybe be the cake specialist – which will be cheaper than buying them in, which is what we usually do. And so, to the accompaniment of Gina G and *Ooh Ahh...Just A Little Bit* on the radio we're all working away, the happy kitchen team of Scott, Lila and me. Scott has perked up a bit and he finds it amusing to have Lila in the kitchen. He grins at me from over in the corner. And then when Sarah comes into the kitchen with a pile of dirty plates she sort of does a double take when she sees little Lila in her whites, fiercely beating the cake mixture with a wooden spoon. 'Oh hello,' she says. 'Do you, er, work here now?' 'Looks like it doesn't it!' says Lila proudly.

It's 3 o' clock now, Lila's cakes are in the oven, the lunchtime rush is over and it's time to get a bit of lunch myself so I help myself to a piece of Donna's quiche, a jacket potato and some salad. I ask Lila if she'd like to join me and so she gets herself a smaller portion of what I'm having and we sit down together at a table at the back of the dining room to eat. And it feels like we're a couple, and people will be starting to see us as such. 'Can we do something tonight?' she says to me. 'Let's go out for a meal.' This is a bit of a development, but why not? 'Okay, yeah, let's celebrate you starting work at the tea shop. Where shall we go?' 'Let's go to the Swinside Inn,' she says, which kind of takes me by surprise, but it's a good idea because it's suddenly got so busy in town this weekend and it might be a bit quieter at the Swinny. Maybe she suggested the Swinny because it's quite near Rigg Beck and she's hoping I'll take her back there. And I feel I ought to take her to the house some time, but I have resisted so far. I don't like the thought of a sleepless night, plus I don't want things to get too serious between us. Another thing is that I suppose I see Rigg Beck as my solitary retreat, my 'castle in the mountains' - as I described it to Sarah one day. I don't mind a friend like Sarah coming up because she's just a friend, but I am wary of having Lila up there. Maybe I'm being mean-spirited and maybe I should invite her back. I look at her sat beside me in that oversized white jacket, the loyal 'girlfriend' who will do anything for me, who is gentle-natured and patient and tolerant of me, tolerant even of my attempt to finish with her the other day – though why should I want to finish with her? If you've got love, why throw it away? She smiles at me. 'What are you thinking?' she says. 'Oh nothing,' I say, but I'm thinking that she seems to be winning me over. 'Yes, let's go to the Swinny.'

After we've had our lunch we go back into the kitchen and she checks on her cakes – but they need a bit longer yet and she asks me what she should do. I scratch my chin and wonder what's best. Nigel only asked her to bake a couple of cakes but now that she's here she might as well do something else. 'How about a dessert for the evening menu? I dunno, maybe a tiramisu. Could you make one of those?' 'Yep, I reckon I can.' 'There should be a recipe in that desserts book over there.' And then I check the fridges to see what prep needs doing for tonight and I see that we need some more chicken curry. I don't really like making the meat dishes if I can help it and so I ask Scott if he'd like to make it. He jumps at the chance to get away from the washing up and do something more creative and so he gets on with that. And I am happy to do the washing up, which gives me a break from the food prep, and I quite enjoy it – I just wish we had a better dishwasher. With this one you have to rinse everything first, and then you have to check everything afterwards and maybe put it through a second time. Then there are the pans and mixing bowls and whatnot that have to be washed by hand. The radio is on a shelf in this corner, and just now it's playing *Firestarter* by Prodigy.

in the boiler room

It gets to four o' clock and it's time to scoot off. Lila's cakes and tiramisu are done and so she knocks off too. I get the key to the boiler room and we both go round to get changed. 'It's been a good afternoon,' I say, and she agrees that it has and she looks pretty happy. Once we're in the boiler room we start getting undressed, and watching her getting undressed makes me feel pretty horny. She's just in her bra under the chef's jacket and a pink thong under the trousers. She's got her back to me as she leans forward to pull the over-sized trousers over her white trainers, and I get a magnificent view of her arse. I cannot help but move forward to grasp it as she's bending over, and she giggles as she fumbles with getting the trousers over her shoes. She turns round to face me and we have a kiss. I've taken my jacket and trousers off and am down to my undies and it feels great to feel her body against mine, flesh against flesh – *hot* flesh because it gets hot in that kitchen and it's even hotter in this boiler room. As we snog I can feel myself sweating and I can feel her own sweat in the small of her back and smell the sweat from her armpits, the musky exciting smell of fresh female sweat. And as we kiss I feel my cock hardening in my briefs and pressing into her, and she can feel it too as she reaches down and cups her hand over it. I pull away from the kiss and turn her round and ask her to bend over so that I can get a view of her backside again. And so she bends over, her hands holding onto the sides of the washing machine to support herself. I remove her bra and play with her tits for a bit and then I move down and my hands are all over her arse, kneading her buttocks and pulling them apart and stroking her cunt through that thin strip of pink cotton fabric. I can see the sweat beading on the pale skin of her back, and a droplet running from her armpit down her skinny arm. And as I keep massaging between her legs I can feel the heat and moisture under the thong. I pull away to take off my briefs and she looks so good, bent over the washing machine in just that bubblegum pink thong and her white trainers and pink anklet socks, waiting for me to take her. I pull the thong to one side and prise open the lips of her juicy little cunt. She sighs. I move up against her and stroke the end of my cock over her wet lips, finally pressing into her, penetrating her, and she sighs again as she feels me going inside her, and she mutters 'oh baby,' and it feels so good to be inside her, to be thrusting into her tight little cunt in this hot boiler room, the sweat running off us both, and this is the best sex with her yet and I have to hold back a little to wait for her pleasure to take over her, and now her cunt is contracting and her legs are trembling and she's whimpering as she clings to the side of the washing machine – which is noisily vibrating as the punters' bed linen spins round at seven hundred revolutions per minute, and I hear myself grunting as I spurt into her again and again, pumping my load into her as I hold onto her hips, the randy chef having his way with the young cake baker, or maybe the boyfriend and girlfriend just doing what boyfriends and girlfriends do. I pull out of her and pull her off the spinning washing machine and we have a tender face-to-face kiss and just hold each other for a little while.

But time marches on and it's time to get dressed and get going and I have to cycle back to Rigg Beck, have a bath and then drive back down here to meet the new chef John and then meet up with Lila later. And so with a quick peck and a 'see you later' I'm on my bike, cycling out of town, my legs feeling a bit weak after the sex – especially when I start climbing the hills coming out of Portinscale. When I get to the Swinny I pause for a moment and consider sitting in the beer garden with a pint of *Stella* for a bit, but decide there isn't time and so on I go, down to Stair, then up the steep hill to join the road from Braithwaite, and back up to Rigg Beck, where I have a quick bath and a cup of tea and get changed. All my clothes are outdoorsy, but since we're going out for a meal later I select my smartest trousers and my new *Patagonia* fleece. Then it's into the burgundy V-dub and into town again.

don't worry, be happy

I get to the restaurant at 5.55pm and change again – back into some whites – and then once I'm in the kitchen Nigel introduces me to John, a muscular fellow with dark long wavy hair, a golden hoop earring, tattoos on his forearms, a tight yellow tee-shirt with the words 'Don't worry, be happy' and a broad smile. We shake hands, and then he goes off to the boiler room to get changed himself. And then the checks start coming in and John and I do them between us. He's actually quite experienced in this game and I'm sure he'll be all right but it's good for him to see the way we do things here, as well as simply to see where things are kept. Scott is over on wash-up as usual and he'll be able to help John later, if it gets busy. Also Nigel says he's going to stay for a bit – out the front with Taz and Emma, to make sure everything's all right, but he says he could also help in the kitchen as well, if needs be (although it's very rare to see him working in the kitchen). John gives me the impression that he doesn't want me to hang around, and he seems confident enough and so at 7.30 I knock off – and it was hardly worth me coming in again really, just to do another hour-and-a-half, but it's all money and I had to come into town anyway – to see Lila.

Dressed in my smart gear I walk round to Windsor House to meet her. She's put some smart gear on too, and even a little make-up – some red lipstick. She looks good, although she's a bit distraught about something. Apparently her best friend Tracy back home in Sunderland has died in a car crash. We sit down together on the edge of the bed and I put my arm around her to comfort her as she cries a little. I don't know what to say. What *can* you say? All I can do is be kind to her and comfort her and be loving I guess. Poor thing, she's had a hard upbringing and some bad luck so far, it seems. She's a vulnerable thing and she needs someone to protect her and be there for her. It could be me, but I'm not sure. I don't think I want to take on the responsibility, to be honest, but then again I'm not ruling out the possibility so we'll see how it goes. Perhaps we could shack up together in the flat at Rigg Beck and be a proper couple? The trouble is she doesn't drive and so it would be hard for her to get in and out of town. And I don't want to live in town anymore – I want to live at Rigg Beck. She doesn't have a job either, apart from part-time cake baker – which will probably only be a few hours a week. I wonder if she really did get sacked from her job at the supermarket. Why would people say that if it wasn't true? To be honest I don't mind if she did get sacked (just for stealing a couple of chocolate bars according to Scott). I wouldn't hold it against her, you know. It's no major crime, and it's possibly a bigger crime for the supermarket to have sacked her. I don't actually know if she was sacked or not, but I don't like the thought of her being dishonest with me. I wish she'd tell me, but she'd probably be too ashamed to admit to being sacked for stealing. If only she knew that I wouldn't be bothered. It's more important to me that she tells the truth. She's stopped crying now. I wipe away a tear from her cheek and give her a kiss and say 'Let's go out.'

And so we get in the car and head out of town to the Swinside Inn. It's unusual having her in the car with me and it reinforces that feeling of us being a proper couple. She reaches over and strokes my leg affectionately as I drive. And when we get to the pub we find that it's very busy, but we are lucky because a couple are just leaving and so we manage to get a table. I raise my pint of Jennings *Cumberland Ale* and she raises her half a *Stella* and I say 'Here's to happy times at the tea shop' and we clink our glasses together. She smiles and sips at her lager and I gulp down a goodly amount of ale – about half of the pint in fact. We peruse the menu and Lila decides that she wants fish and chips with mushy peas. Okay, she's not a real vegetarian, she's a *pescatarian*, or 'pesky' for short, and I'm a pesky too if the truth be told. I have been a strict vegetarian and even thought about going vegan, but it's difficult when you go out for a meal like this and usually the only veggie options are things that have been bought in frozen from Brake Brothers or some other supplier, things like spinach and ricotta cannelloni which have been defrosted and microwaved to death and then been transferred into a serving dish and maybe browned a bit on top under the grill. But on the specials board there is a home-made vegetable pie served with new potatoes and vegetables of the day and I decide to plump for one of those. I go to the bar to place our order and decide that I might as well get another pint, whilst I'm at it. I look around me and I like this place – a traditional old-fashioned Lakeland pub, with an ancient-looking oak cabinet against one wall, and an open fire. It's 8.40 pm now and I suspect that food orders will have died off a bit and we won't have to wait too long. I rejoin Lila at our table and we have a drink and we talk about the tea shop for a bit. 'Do you think I could get a full-time job there?' she says. 'I dunno love, but I do know that people are always leaving, especially from the kitchen. It's a pretty disorganised place, not very professional I suppose, and some people can't get on with that. Anyway, now that you've got your foot in the door...you never know.' 'I want to be a chef,' she says. 'Maybe you should go to catering college,' I say. 'If you're qualified you can earn more. Paul is college-trained. I think he probably left because the other place is paying him more.' And we talk about the tea shop and the people there and then our food arrives at 9.15pm and we're both hungry and so we concentrate on eating. 'How's yer fish?' I ask. 'Good, it's cooked just right. Nice crispy batter. How's yer pie?' 'Aye, it's good too.' The 'vegetables of the day' with the pie are carrots and broccoli. The carrots have just been peeled, topped and tailed and boiled whole. I guess the chef has done this just to save time, but I think they look good and taste good like this, so maybe it's something I might try at the tea shop, as long as Nigel approves - which he probably won't, now I think about it. I get a bit tired of talking about the tea shop with Lila, although she is interested to hear all about it. I rack my brains for other things to talk about, but can't come up with much. I don't want to ask her about her friend Tracy in case she gets upset again, and I don't really want to question her about the supermarket either. So what shall we talk about? To tell the truth we don't have much common ground, and although I said before that it felt like we were a proper couple, that feeling didn't last long, and my feeling now is the usual one of there being quite a distance between us. We hold hands for a bit but to me it feels like we're just going through the motions.

By 10.30 pm I'm feeling pretty tired and I suggest we go, and so I pay up and we leave. As we walk to the car Lila says that she'd like to see the Purple House some time. 'Yeah, come round some time,' I say. 'But not tonight. I'm too tired.' I drive back into town and drop her off at Windsor House and kiss her goodnight and then drive back the same way, past the Swinny and back to Rigg Beck. I go up to my room, get a can of lager from the fridge, put a CD on the stereo and sit in one of the red armchairs. The CD is *Jagged Little Pill* by Alanis Morissette. Matt from the tea shop taped this for me, but I liked it so much I decided to buy the CD. (So there you are Emma, the taping actually had the effect of gaining a sale for Alanis Morissette, so nothing morally dodgy there).

The first track, *All I Really Want* comes on and her shrill voice is a bit mad and a bit hard on the ears at first, but once you're used to it it's great. She says a line that sounds like 'I'd like a *Stella*', which makes me smile as I like a *Stella* myself and am drinking one right now. I would quote you the line she sings but the law forbids me from quoting any song lyrics. It's only three words, but if I quote them verbatim then Alanis or her publisher might come down on me like a ton of bricks and take me to court for everything I'm worth – which is actually very little, in fact less than zero because all I've got is debts and so maybe I should just go ahead and quote her lyrics, and the lyrics of songs by other artists that I'd like to quote in this book, although to be honest I suppose I don't really need to. Anyway, I wonder if Alanis would like to join me with a *Stella*. I look at her face on the CD cover and she's a good-looking gal and she could go down on me in a theatre any time she likes, except that I never *go* to the theatre. And I reckon that most people who say they like going to the theatre like the *idea* of it more than the actual experience. It's what it connotes. It is definitely a badge of middle-classification – is it not? And Alanis, for all her neurotic angry screeching is essentially middle-class, the educated middle-class bad girl, or would-be bad girl. Certainly the boyfriends she's had in her songs are middle-class, with their golf-playing and their single malt whisky. She's maybe going through a phase and she'll grow out of it and find her soul mate and settle down and have kids... And what *I* wouldn't give to find a soulmate, a 'kindred'... Lila is working-class and not fucked up by education and middle-class neuroses, although she's fucked up in other ways, so I am learning...and she aint my soul mate. Maybe I was being a bit harsh on Alanis there, and maybe I'd be better suited to going out with someone like her rather than Lila. Alanis says that she needs some intellectual intercourse, and that's what I need too. And I reckon we could have a good conversation. She's intelligent, creative, and a free spirit. Yeah, I reckon we could talk about 'life' for a while. I look at her photo on the cover again. She's got long dark hair, strong features, and an American look about her. When she sings her American accent comes through strongly. And she's a strong woman. Strong, independent, feisty. Actually I think she's Canadian, so she might even appreciate the architecture of Rigg Beck. We could sit on the verandah together and swap life-stories whilst drinking Chardonnay, and she might tell me that it was actually her grandfather who built this house. Now wouldn't that be ironic, don't you think? A little too ironic...or maybe not.

I'm very tired now and I'll have to go to bed soon. I swig down the last of the lager then brush my teeth at the sink. Then I turn down the volume and turn off the main light, and with the soft light from the lamp on the bedside table I listen to a bit more Alanis. I'm back at the tea shop tomorrow for breakfasts and the day shift and then I've got a couple of days off, which is good because I feel like I need some time to take stock of things.

up in the clouds

Running now up Skiddaw in the drizzling rain, it's a day off from the tea shop, and it's been a week since that meal at the Swinny with Lila. I like running up and down Skiddaw on the main tourist path because it's runnable all the way and you can do it on a bad weather day. You don't have to worry about navigation, it's just one foot in front of the other on this slatey treadmill and all you have to think about is keeping it going...and as I'm working my way up Jenkin Hill now, into the clag, this is the steepest bit and if I was to break into a hands-on-knees style walk I could probably move forwards and upwards just as fast, but I'd rather keep the momentum going, the rhythm of the running. There are no views now, just the ground beneath my feet and the thick grey cloud ahead. Now and then walkers loom out of the clag, some of them coming towards me, others going up like me – and there are quite a lot of them, despite the bad weather, Skiddaw being a popular mountain.

I'm feeling pretty tired to be honest – tired from working at the tea shop and probably also tired from being with Lila. And I'm not sure I believe those ideas about sexual energy and spiritual energy because today my life-force feels a bit depleted. Maybe it's the cumulative tiredness from the tea shop and also that the sex with Lila has become routine and has lost its spark. I tried to finish with her again this week but she just had to offer up her body and I couldn't say no and we're still together. She keeps coming up with these tall stories and I don't think she's being honest with me. The other day – the day after I tried to finish with her – I went round to her house and her stuff from the wardrobe was all over the floor. She said the police had been round and ransacked the place looking for drugs and she was all upset about it and I had to comfort her and go along with it, but it was a bit weird to say the least. I mean she's no drug user and, as far as I know, she doesn't associate with anyone who is. She also reckoned that the police have some sort of surveillance operation in progress at the back of the tea shop – which is actually plausible since a lot of buying and selling seems to go on there. Half the staff at the tea shop are regular cannabis users, and one day I saw the new chef John cutting up a block of the stuff in the kitchen. Anyway, back to Lila... I'm starting to have suspicions that she's some kind of compulsive liar. I can't believe that she really is a published short story writer for instance. (She said she'd been on the phone to her agent, and that she's had a couple more stories accepted for magazines.) And that business with the cat was strange. When the owner saw me going up to Windsor House the other day she called over to me and told me that Lila had stolen her cat and that Lila was always getting into trouble and that I shouldn't have anything to do with her. I thought that was none of her business. Lila is 'my girl', just about, and I have to stand by her, but things are starting to get a bit strained. Another thing is that her housemate Anna came into the tea shop one day and was complaining to me that Lila keeps leaving the kitchen in a mess and that she's behind with her rent and she's in danger of being kicked out. Well I might be 'seeing' her, but I'm not responsible for her. And I don't want to be tarred with the same brush when she upsets people. By the way, talking of Anna reminds me that Mrs Vee told me that Anna's two sisters are going to move into Rigg Beck and buy the house – in August probably. If that's true I may have to move out, although I don't know where to. But it might not happen... I know lots of people have talked about buying Rigg Beck but for some reason it doesn't happen. Maybe when they look closely at all the work that needs to be done they change their minds. Or maybe Mrs Vee decides that she aint selling after all. A few years ago it was Anna's adoptive mother who was talking about buying the house but it didn't happen. I don't know where these people get their money from. The two sisters don't work and they're only young – younger than me. It must be family money, inherited money, trust funds or some such. Before Mrs Vee told me this I'd been making plans to stay at the house over the winter and do loads of writing, and she said she'd reduce my rent a bit if I would stay over the winter, but now everything's up in the air – as it so often is in my life.

Up in the clouds right now I've got to the top of the steep climb up Jenkin Hill, and I'm feeling stronger now that I've managed to keep the momentum going up the steep hard bit, and I can stretch my legs and pick up the pace as I trot up this gentle climb. And then it's through a gate and round the back of Skiddaw Little Man on a level contouring track, and I can really stretch out along here. Then it gets steeper as I approach the bulk of Skiddaw herself, and it's through another gate and the steep climb up onto the ridge – where it's a lot windier (and it always seems to be very windy up here) and I'm picking my way through the rocks to the summit, where there is a trig point, a shelter and a circular slate viewpoint thing with the names of all the fells engraved into the surface – all the fells that you can see on a clear day when you can see for miles, but today in this cloud you can only see about ten yards in front of you and so without any pause I run round the trig point and start the run back down the same way I came. And once I'm off the summit ridge it's an exhilarating descent, running as fast as I can, down, down, cutting the corner of Jenkin Hill through the tussocky grass, then back on the slatey path, and suddenly I'm out of the cloud and I can see the car park by Latrigg, and to the right of that – the grey stone buildings of the town, and Derwentwater and Borrowdale stretching into the distance. I bound down the short grass beside the fence, up the little rise, past the monument, through the car park, then the winding track through the trees down Latrigg, going hell for leather – for the hell of it, walkers coming up giving me a wide berth, which I acknowledge with a wave of my hand, and then it's over the bridge over the A66 to Briar Rigg, where my car is parked under the trees. And I check my stopwatch: 1 hr 19 mins. I've done it faster, but that's not bad for a training run – a training run on a grey wet day.

a sort of mandala

Painting in the kitchen at Rigg Beck I am totally absorbed in this work I am creating – a chaos of reds and some purple, brushstrokes criss-crossing each other, trying to keep a balance, a pattern across the square board. The focal point is the centre, where the colour is lightest, with strands radiating out to the edge, which is darker. A sort of abstract sunburst, perhaps. I'm not referring to anything exterior, just what's inside my head, and for a while I'm in a trance.

I recently got into doing these abstract expressionist 'action' paintings, inspired by the work of Jackson Pollock – although my technique is different, and they look quite different. I like the intricate patterns that Pollock created with his drips of paint. They suggest to me a mystical vision of interconnectedness, a vision that I want to express in my own creativity. I also like the vigour, the energy in his paintings, and so I decided to have a go myself.

I've bought these pieces of hardboard from the DIY store in town, cut them into squares of between one foot and three foot in size, and then primed them with white emulsion paint. And then of an evening, when the feeling takes me, I set to work with my acrylics, painting on the kitchen table with some music on and some beer on the go. The idea is that I work fast and complete the painting in one sitting, which usually takes a couple of hours. And what I paint usually just comes straight out of my head. I generally have some idea of what colour combinations I want to use – the other day it was variations of green and purple – and I try to build up some kind of pattern, sometimes with a central focal point, and sometimes with no focal point at all. I've been disappointed with the ones I've done so far – which have ended up being a muddy mess. I think maybe I'm using the wrong type of paint for what I want to do, or at least applying it too thickly. Thick acrylic paint is not really suitable for working fast on an action painting. But tonight I've thinned it right down so that it's working more like watercolour and the result is much better. One thing about doing this sort of painting is knowing when to stop because if you do too much you can ruin it, and you can't get it back to the way it was before. I think I've reached that stopping point just now... I stand back to look at what I've produced and I'm pleased with it, *very* pleased in fact. The balance of colours and interwoven brush strokes is just right. There is a symmetry, an orderliness and a cleanliness to the piece. To me there is something *spiritual* about it; it's a sort of *mandala*.

Another painting idea I've had is to do a large piece based on the one inch Ordnance Survey map of the Lake District. This too would be a sort of *mandala* for me. I used to have this map on my bedroom wall at home, years before I moved to the Lakes and when I was still at school in fact. I was fascinated by the area and avidly reading Wainwright's guides and going there fellwalking at every opportunity. (I lived in Merseyside, so not too far away.) The map made a good picture on the wall, picking out the shape of the ridges with its shading and the lakes radiating from a central point – which might be Grasmere, or High Raise. There was something symmetrical, ordered and special about the layout of the land. Even as a teenager I vaguely dreamed about making an epic journey, a round of the Lakeland Fells, long before I'd ever heard of the Bob Graham Round. Anyway this painting idea is something for the future perhaps...

I prop my red abstract sunburst on top of the fridge and admire it from a distance. It's a Rigg Beck tradition for artists to leave a painting for the house, which is usually a painting *of* the house – and there are a few on the wall going down the staircase – and so I think I'll donate this one. I might not be doing much writing at the moment, but at least I am doing some painting, and there seems to be something about this house that is conducive to creativity of one sort or another.

comrades in arms

Driving into town to do the breakfasts at the tea shop, it's a grey morning, but calm and dry. I'm feeling quite good after my two days off, spent mostly on my own – running, reading and painting. I didn't see Lila because she went away, back home to Sunderland for a few days, though she's coming back today.

I let myself in at the back door of the tea shop and the first thing I notice is a really bad smell. I don't know what it is – rotting food or something. I walk into the kitchen and the place is in complete disarray – unwashed pots and pans everywhere, piled up on every work surface and even dumped on the floor by the dishwasher. The floor is filthy with dirty marks and bits of food everywhere. Also there are lots of empty *Becks* beer bottles all over the place. Next to the cooker there's a slip of paper with the breakfast choices written in Taz's handwriting: '6 x full'. I can't believe what a mess the place is in. I've never seen anything like it. God knows what happened last night. But what's that disgusting smell? I walk over to the fridge and the smell gets stronger and I see a couple of chicken portions sitting in a pool of blood on a plate on top of the fridge. The blood has overflowed the plate and run down the back of the fridge, and it smells absolutely disgusting. I wonder how long it's been there. Longer than just overnight I reckon. I feel angry. What kind of a stupid fucking place is this! It's ridiculous! I light the oven, switch the radio on and start to get the breakfast ingredients together – but before I can start cooking I have to wash a couple of pans for the mushrooms and beans. I'll probably have to wash some plates and cutlery too. On the radio it's The Fugees and *Ready Or Not*. I get the breakfasts cooked and served, and as I take them into the dining room I wonder if the punters can smell that horrible smell from the chicken portions. Maybe I should just throw them away, but I didn't put them there and Scott can deal with it when he comes in.

At 9 o' clock Sarah comes in, but not Scott. Sarah is appalled by the mess and stink in the kitchen and she shakes her head and says 'I'm sick of this place.' I phone Nigel to tell him about the kitchen and Scott not turning in and he says he'll be in himself in about an hour. I take ten minutes to have a coffee with Sarah and we both have a good moan about what a ridiculous place this is and that makes us feel better. She's a comrade in arms is Sarah and she has a similar take on things to me and I'm glad she works here. She's a friend. She reminds me that she wants to come and visit me at Rigg Beck some time and I say 'Yeah, come up one evening after work, and I'll cook you a meal.' 'Okay, I look forward to it.'

As we're sat at the table, chatting away, Taz comes in through the front door to see us. She's on her way to a massage appointment, but she thought she'd just drop by to let us know what happened last night. 'Scott kept helping himself to bottles of *Becks* and he got very drunk. John was drinking too, and they were even smoking weed in the kitchen. It was very busy with orders and John kept making mistakes and there were loads of complaints and it was very embarrassing. Scott disappeared at 9 'o clock and then so did John shortly afterwards. Sorry I didn't do any washing up, but I had enough to do waiting on.' 'That's all right Taz, it's not your job to do the washing up.'

I go back into the kitchen and wonder where to start. First I need to check the fridges to see what we've got. It's likely to be busy today; there are lots of people in town for the annual Keswick Christian Convention. I check the back fridge – which is where we generally keep most of the stuff we've prepped up. It's been running too warm now for a couple of weeks and Nigel knows about it but hasn't done anything about it. No doubt he thinks we'll get away with it and he doesn't want the expense of calling out an engineer or buying a new one. I open the door and I am greeted with a draft of warm air. Actually *warm*. Shit! I check the thermometer and it's showing 17 degrees C.

There's a big plastic tub of veg soup with no cling film over it and there are these bubbles on top, like it's fermenting. And there is a stink of the mixture of all kinds of things, vegetable and meat dishes in plastic tubs – all going off. Bacteria will be breeding like wild fire and we can't use any of this. Knowing Nigel he'd probably say some of it will be all right but I don't want to take the risk. I'm in charge of the kitchen today and I don't want to be responsible for poisoning someone, so I start throwing stuff away. Most of it will have to go in a plastic bin bag; the soup I'll pour down the drain outside the back door. There is so much to do and there's no way we're going to be able to offer the usual menu tonight.

Around 11 o'clock Nigel walks into the kitchen and he's in a foul mood. He says that John's left and he can't get hold of Scott. He starts sniffing the air. 'What's *that*?' And then he sees the chicken on top of the fridge. 'Get rid of it!' I show him the warm fridge and he starts shouting and swearing. 'Fuck! What have I done to deserve this! Who's going to leave next? Are *you* going to leave next?' And I'm thinking yeah Nigel, the way things are going I might just do that because I'm totally pissed off with this place and I have no faith in your management of it. But I'm going to have to carry on for the time being... He walks over to the dishwasher, surveys the piles of unwashed pots and pans and shakes his head. Above the dishwasher on the shelf the radio is playing *Loser* by Beck. 'Fuck off!' snarls Nigel. He reaches up, unplugs the radio, picks it up and stomps out of the kitchen with it, red-faced and fuming. And I am left to get on with preparing what I can for the lunchtime menu, with no Scott and no tunes to keep me company.

I can hear Nigel having a go at Sarah now in the dining room. I can't make out everything he's saying, but I hear his raised voice saying 'Just get on with it!' and then I hear the front door slam as he leaves and Sarah appears at the kitchen doorway with tears in her eyes, her bottom lip quivering. 'Come here Sarah' I say, and she walks up to me and I put my arm around her and she cries on my shoulder. 'The bastard!' she says, in between sobs. 'Yes, he *is* a bastard.' Fortunately there are no customers in just now and Sarah can have a cry for five minutes. I rub her back affectionately and say 'We'll have to leave this place.' 'You're telling me!' she says. The tears stop and she wipes her eyes with a paper tissue, gives me a smile and then goes out the back door to have a roll-up cigarette. 'Give me a shout if anyone comes in' she says, but no-one comes in and she can enjoy her smoke.

At twelve noon we get the first of our lunchers, and also a lad called 'Frog' walks into the kitchen and says he's come to do the washing up. He's dressed pretty scruffily and he's got these thick glasses and an intelligent look about him. He pitches straight into the washing up and I can see he's no slacker. He tells me he's a local, a Keswickian, and he's just got back from travelling round Europe in a van and he needs work, any kind of work for some cash. He's got a VW Transporter van which he's been living in for the last twelve months and he's parked up in the 'quarry' near Rigg Beck. Well fancy that – I've seen this van parked there the last couple of days and wondered whose it was. The quarry is an actual disused roadside quarry - now a small parking area - just down from the bridge over the beck, where fellwalkers park up before setting off on their walk, and sometimes you do get travelling types who park up there for a few days. Frog tells me he was thinking of asking Mrs Vee for a room in the house, but he's so used to sleeping in his van he's happy to carry on doing that. He finds sleeping in buildings claustrophobic by comparison, although he's thinking it will be useful to pay some minimal rent to Mrs Vee so that he can use the bathroom and kitchen. And I take my hat off to him as someone who can live so simply, with very few possessions – although if the truth be told he's probably got a lot of gear stored at his parents' house in town and he can go there any time he likes for a hot meal and a hot shower.

It does get quite busy over the lunchtime period, but we cope okay. I managed to knock up some tomato and basil soup and I put some jacket potatoes in the oven, and most of the lunchtime bits and bobs are kept in the fridge that's still working so things aint too bad after all. We are low on mixed salad and I have to keep breaking off from orders to chop away and try and build up a reserve of that. I have a quick sandwich on the job at about 2 o' clock and then start making a list of all the things that have to be made for the evening menu. And I wonder where we are going to store it all because we don't have the fridge space anymore. Well, that's for Nigel to sort out... I get on with making a load of chick pea chilli.

Around 4 o' clock Lila appears at the back door, looking distraught. 'I've been kicked out the house,' she says. 'What? Why?' 'I don't know...for no reason. I just got back and Jim's changed the locks on my door and I have to move out *today*.' 'Where are you going to go? What are you going to do?' 'My friend says I can stay at her place in town for the time being, but it's only temporary. Maybe I could live at Rigg Beck?' 'I don't know... I'll come round to Windsor House in an hour to see you – will you be there?' 'Yes, I'll be a while packing my stuff... My friend's got a car so she can help me move.'

we all need a home

And so at 5 o' clock I finish the day shift at the tea shop and walk round to see Lila at the house. I ring the bell and the landlord Jim comes to the door. 'I've come to see Lila,' I say. 'Oh you're with *her* are you? She's nothing but trouble and she owes me six weeks' rent and she's moving out...' He lets me in and I go down the corridor to Lila's room. And it's such a sad sight, the poor girl being evicted from her place, her possessions piled up in boxes and bags, and I've been in the same situation myself and it's tragic really. We all need a home, but if you can't pay the rent you can't have one. What are you supposed to do? Live on the streets or in a cave? The people that let rooms don't care about that - all they are interested in is the money, and if it aint forthcoming you are out on your arse. Of course I can understand it from the landlord's point of view too – they want the rent income for paying the bills and the upkeep of the house and to maintain a certain standard of living to which they have become accustomed. But they are in this privileged position, this position of power over someone's basic need for shelter, a bed, somewhere to store their stuff, somewhere to wash and cook etc. They never see it from the tenant's position. They are lucky enough to own a large 'property' and they want to maximise what income they can get from letting rooms, and if you renege on the agreement, the contract, then it's out the door you go and who cares what happens to you because you are a non-payer, a 'criminal' for having no money and not providing him with the income to pay for another ski-ing holiday or whatever. It's the powerful versus the vulnerable, and the powerful aint interested in vulnerability, they are only interested in the contract, the bottom line, the *money*. Okay, maybe Lila had been a troublesome tenant apart from not paying her rent. She was always leaving the kitchen in a mess, she'd upset Anna, she'd stolen someone's cat, she was a shoplifter and a liar, but she is also a vulnerable young person who was abused as a child and it's not true to say that she's 'nothing but trouble' because she has her good points – she's warm, friendly, generous, kind, and she wants to give – as a lover, as an employee, as a social person, as a human being. And now here is another door being slammed in her face and she's having to try and maintain some dignity in the situation. I could take her under my wing but I know it wouldn't work - I can't be her social worker, I've got enough problems of my own. I'm not exactly in a stable situation and I'm not exactly a stable person myself. There is no way I want her to live with me at Rigg Beck. It definitely wouldn't work. I feel sorry for her, but also a bit angry with her for being dishonest with me. Maybe she can't help telling lies but it's no good being lied to all the time – you can't trust a person, and any relationship has got to be based on trust. The friend who is with her is Tracy, the one who is supposed to have died. She's just moved to Keswick and got herself a job at the Italian restaurant and a small flat. She says to me 'She'll be all right. She can live with me, and I'll try and get her a job where I work.' That's what friends are for. And girls are generally better at 'being there' for their friends than men are. This is crunch time and I know that it's definitely over between me and Lila. It shouldn't be such a big deal – I mean we've only been seeing each other for a couple of months, and not seriously, but I do feel a bit bad about it as I walk away. Sometimes it seems it's best not to get involved with people who you're not sure about – and maybe Pat was right – but then how can you *not* get involved? I don't want to spend my life avoiding life and I am grateful if someone shows an interest in me, no matter who they are. Perhaps, as Nietzsche said 'the solitary extends his hand too readily', but then again I think it's a good thing to extend the hand to anyone and everyone, with no snobbery, no sense of superiority or inferiority or even of much *difference*. We are all equal under the eyes of God, we are all human and all from the same stock, with the same basic needs and feelings, and it's surely a good thing to get to know lots of different kinds of people. A truly religious goal in life would be to get to know as many different people as possible. And by 'getting to know' of course I mean *really* getting to know and *understanding* them. Such are my thoughts as I walk down Lake Road for a breather, before I head back to the tea shop to start the evening shift.

flesh and blood

Back in the kitchen, Pat is here to help me for the evening. He's made up a load of mixture for the mushroom tag so we can offer that or chick pea chilli for the vegetarians. We haven't actually got anything to offer the meat-eaters as the meat was kept in the fridge that broke down. So it looks like we're back to being a vegetarian establishment tonight – with just two main dishes on the menu. Actually I think we'll have to try and offer some things from the daytime menu as well, though I don't know what. Salads and jacket potatoes I suppose. That's just the way it'll have to be, and it'll make our job easier, and both Pat and I are vegetarians so we are happy not to be cooking meat.

We have quite an easy evening between us, taking it in turns to do the orders and the washing up, although there aren't actually many orders (and therefore not much washing up) because when punters walk through the door and Taz tells them we've only got two dishes on offer (both vegetarian) many of them turn round and go back out the door. By nine 'o clock the dining room is empty and all the washing up is done, the floor is swept and mopped and we've even scrubbed the hob so that it's cleaner than it's ever been. Time to go for some beers...and Pat and I get changed and head for The Cellar Bar.

Over a *Bitburger* Pat tells me that he wants to be a yoga teacher. He's got some contact on a Greek island and he's hoping to head out there pretty soon. He actually leaves the job at the tea shop on Thursday – in a couple of days' time. I wonder why he came to work at the tea shop in the first place. I think he saw the place advertised in a vegetarian guide and thought he'd like to give it a go and spend a summer in the Lakes. So he just pitched up and more or less said 'gis a job' and Nigel said 'okay'. He was a bit disappointed that the place wasn't actually vegetarian anymore, but hey ho it was still worth a go. Like me he's not a 'proper' chef, not a *qualified* chef, so Nigel pays us less than what he paid Paul or John for instance – not that either of those two were any good, especially John (and I'm not convinced that John was qualified anyway).

Talking of Paul, here he comes now, coming to join us. He's just finished his shift at the kitchen in this place, where he now works. He says he's been really busy, what with the Convention crowd, and tells us some figure of how many meals he's done, which is supposed to impress us. 'We've done nowt at the tea shop,' I say, and tell him about the chaos with John leaving, Scott not turning in, the fridge breaking down etcetera etcetera. 'Do you know where Scott is?' I ask him. He doesn't know but says that he's probably 'gone walkabout', which is something he does from time to time. 'He's mebbe gone over to Newcastle...he's got friends there. But he'll be back.' And so we chat for a while about what a mad place the tea shop is and then he invites us back to his place 'for a smoke'. His place is actually Donna's place, as he's lodging with her now – in that box room where I briefly stayed myself. Donna is away with the kids and he's got the place to himself.

We drink more beer at The Cellar Bar before going to Donna's house, and I'm conscious that I'm knocking it back faster than usual. I guess it's been a stressful day, what with the chaos at the tea shop and finally splitting with Lila. And I feel a bit drunk as we walk up Main Street, and wanting to drink more. At Donna's Paul puts on some music – the Oasis album *(What's The Story) Morning Glory* – and gets some cans of lager from the fridge. Pat isn't bothered about drinking much more, although he's keen to smoke a bit of the old wacky baccy. Paul produces this bong and gets it going and he and Pat start imbibing the stuff. Paul offers it to me and I hesitate... It's not the sort of thing I usually do, but because I'm feeling a bit drunk and feeling the need to blow my mind somehow I decide to partake of the stuff and so I suck on the tube and inhale the evil smoke and hold it down as long as I can before exhaling through my nostrils and mouth. Paul is banging on about what a difficult childhood he had and how it's made him self-destructive with drink and drugs. And I'm thinking to myself that too many people play that card nowadays. Lila had a hard childhood and her father sexually abused her as a child, but she didn't go on about how unfortunate she was – though no doubt it had a bad effect on her. It was maybe the root cause of her shoplifting and her lying, and maybe it had something to do with her clinging to me, the mature boyfriend, the father figure. It made her vulnerable, insecure and desperate to find love through sex. And I too had a difficult upbringing. I wasn't physically abused but I had a bad relationship with my father from adolescence onwards. He kicked me out when I was nineteen, after I'd dropped out of college. I'd 'wasted' the money he'd spent on making up my university grant, then on returning home I'd only managed to stick at a labouring job for a week. I think he saw me as a waster and he just wanted to get rid of me. As soon as I'd gone he turned my room into his office, so there was no possibility of me going back. He maybe had a chip on his shoulder because he didn't have the opportunity to go to college himself, he had to go out to work in a factory at the age of fifteen, when his parents split up, and he didn't get on with his step-dad and he had to make his own way in the world from an early age, and then he met my mum (who also had a dysfunctional upbringing) and they had me and my sister when they were relatively young, and then he resented not having been able to go to art college and live a bit before settling down with a wife and kids and mortgage. And I think there was something about me that he just didn't like, even if I was his own 'flesh and blood'. There was something about me that he saw as a threat to his authority – and he was an authoritarian, given towards psychological violence toward his wife and children, and on the night he told me he wanted me out that violence was starting to get physical. To what extent my childhood has affected the way I am today I don't know. No doubt it's had some effect, but I don't use it as an excuse for my problems, and I take full responsibility for the way I live my life. And anyway, what family isn't dysfunctional? The nuclear family is an outmoded and dysfunctional social unit that produces dysfunctional human beings. And if there's ever going to be a New Age, an age in which society is organised in a more enlightened way, then it will be based around *communes*, with child-rearing shared by a number of parent figures – a bit like the old extended family perhaps, but moving away from the supposed importance of one's 'own' offspring. Surely this would produce happier and more emotionally mature individuals...

I feel dizzy and also a bit sick from inhaling the smoke. That feeling passes and suddenly the drug hits me and my mind goes warm and gooey and I find myself laughing at some joke of Paul's that isn't even funny. And the three of us end up giggling like a bunch of retards and we don't even know why we're laughing but it feels good and it's a release from the stresses and strains of the day to have a good laugh. But I'm not going to completely lose myself because I've got to get home to Rigg Beck, and then it's another day in the tea shop... And so after an hour or so of yakking away about god-knows-what I announce that I am going to 'make tracks'. Paul says I can stay the night at Donna's, and that's what Pat is going to do, but I want to get to bed soon and I want my 'own' bed and so I leave them to it and walk back through town to the tea shop.

I'm feeling a bit affected by the beer and the smoke but I reckon I'll be all right driving back, as long as I take it easy. And so away I go, taking it easy at first as I head out of town. As I turn off the A66 at Portinscale I look in the mirror and see the lights of a car behind me also turning off here – and I think it might be a police car (although all I can see is the headlights). It continues behind me through the village and I start to panic a bit and so once I'm through the village I put my foot down and open up a gap between us. I'm driving like a maniac now, really working the car hard up the hills and throwing it round the bends. As I take the turn off for the Swinny I glance in the mirror and I don't see any lights behind me anymore, but once I'm past the pub I pick up the pace again and shoot down to Stair – where I narrowly miss running over a cat or something that runs across the road – then up the hill and back to Rigg Beck. I get out and feel relieved to have made it back in one piece. There are no lights coming up the road. I breathe in the cold evening air and stare at the clear star-speckled sky for a bit, then go into the house and go straight to bed.

worms in the water

Today is Monday, the first of my two days off – and much needed after a week of hell at the tea shop. I've been working evenings as well as day shifts and it's been pretty knackering. Scott came back, all apologetic, and is reinstated in the kitchen. Nigel got an engineer out to look at the fridge and it's now repaired and properly working again. Pat left the job and he moved out of the house on Friday. A new evening chef, Drew, is starting whilst I'm on my days off. He's a stockily-built Scotsman with a professional air about him and Nigel says he's got a good CV, so fingers crossed...

I had a bit of a lie-in this morning, and then when I got up to go to the sink for a wash and shave I turned the tap and all these little worms came out in the water. It was horrible! I got dressed and walked up the beck to the holding tank, where I removed a slab of stone to take a look but couldn't see anything. I walked up the fellside, following the feeder stream, until I came to a dead sheep lying in the stream. It must have been there a few days; it was bloated and stinking in the warm sun. I pulled it out the water and dragged it some distance away and left it lying in the bracken and then walked up the road to tell Craig, the farmer at Birk Rigg. And then I went back to the house and ran the tap again. Worms were still coming out and so I ran the water into a jam jar, put the lid on and went down to the basement to show Mrs Vee. She was a bit concerned, but also found it quite funny. She said that when she moved into the house some thirty-five years ago she secured a piece of an old pair of her nylon tights with a rubber band over the pipe from the water tank – as a filter. 'I don't suppose it's still in place!' she said. After spending a bit of time listening to a Mrs Vee monologue, reminiscing about the house, I set off up the beck again with the jam jar, as I'd noticed earlier that there was what looked like a bunch of students on a Geography field trip or something. They were taking samples of water from the beck and making notes. I went up to the teacher, who told me they were ecologists, and I showed him my jam jar and he said 'Threadworms.' I explained that they were coming out the tap in the house and told him about the dead sheep and he said 'Don't worry, they're completely harmless.' Well harmless they may be, but I don't want then swimming around my mouth or stomach if I take a drink of water, and so when I went into town later to the supermarket I bought a couple of extra large bottles of mineral water.

When I got back from town I went for a short run up the beck and back over Ard Crags, and then went to have a bath. I ran the taps and lo and behold a load of threadworms came out and the bath water was swimming in them. It was disgusting. I couldn't have a bath in that! And so I took my towel and had a walk up the beck, beyond the holding tank and the ecologists to a secluded deepish pool, where I stripped off and had a bath au naturelle in the freezing cold beck water. It's been a warm sunny day, so not a bad day to be doing such a thing, but I was still shivering like mad when I got out.

Now it's late afternoon and I'm sitting on the verandah in the sun, waiting for Sarah to arrive. And I'm thinking I've got to leave this place. I can't be doing with worms coming out in the water. Hopefully the worms will pass, sooner rather than later. The ecologist guy said it would probably only last a day or two. And I'm thinking I've got to leave the tea shop too. That place goes from bad to worse and it's doing my head in. I feel like I've not got enough time to live. It's a manic energy-sapping treadmill and I haven't got the time or energy to do anything much except to try and recover from it on my days off. It's been a particularly hard week, with having to work evenings as well as days, but things should get better now that Drew has started... But the place is so disorganised and I've got no faith in Nigel and I'll probably get made redundant at the end of the season anyway, so I've got to find something else - to which end I'm going for an interview at The Dog and Gun in town tomorrow. But at least right now I am off the treadmill for a couple of days and I'm basking in the warm late-afternoon sun at this idyllic spot.

my home entertainment

Here comes Sarah's car now, a Mini Metro, and she pulls up in front of my car and gets out, all smiling and with a plastic carrier bag containing cans of lager and packets of crisps. She's been working at the tea shop today, and she's come straight here. She sits down on the purple bench beside me and says 'Isn't this lovely!' And it *is* a lovely spot, especially on a warm summer's evening, when it's busy and noisy in town but it's nice and tranquil up here. She produces the cold cans of lager and the crisps and we drink from the can and she asks me about my day and tells me about her day at the tea shop. The new chef Drew did the day shift at the tea shop today and apparently he's okay - pretty tidy, organised and efficient. Scott found the radio in a store cupboard upstairs and put it back in the kitchen, but then when Nigel came in at four o' clock and saw it he threw a tantrum, took it down, stamped on it to break it and then threw it in a skip at the garage. Sarah laughs, and I laugh too. The guy is insane and neither of us want to work for him for much longer. There are quite a few other jobs going in town, but it's a question of finding something suitable. Sarah is a bit like me – ex-uni, ex-YHA and a bit of a misfit. She's got a boyfriend, and he's still working for the YHA in South Lakes but they don't seem very close. They get together sometimes to go walking when their days off coincide but it doesn't exactly seem to be 'full on'. And she seems to be pretty independent, a free spirit who will do her own thing, boyfriend or not.

A car driving up the road slows right down and stops in front of us. The young female passenger smiles over to us from the open window. 'Wow, I love your house!' 'It's pretty cool, isn't it,' I say. 'It sure is,' she says, and they drive off. This is what you get living at Rigg Beck. Usually the cars only pause and people just gawp rather than saying anything. Some of them love the look of the house, and others are curious but appalled at the 'gaudy monstrosity' or whatever. Whichever view you take there's no getting away from the fact that the place is *different*. This is not typical Lake District architecture; this is not a twee white-washed vernacular stone farmhouse; this is more like that house in the film *Psycho*.

After we've supped some lager and eaten the crisps and the sun has dipped below Causey Pike we head indoors and go up to the kitchen. I get the CD player from my room and put on an old-school blues compilation album. And whilst Sarah sits at the table and reads *The Keswick Reminder* I get on with cooking up a curry. Mrs Vee comes up and sticks her head round the door, though I don't know what for. Just being nosy perhaps. I introduce her to Sarah, they exchange pleasantries for a while, and then Mrs Vee says to me 'I'll leave you two alone – I didn't know you had your girlfriend here', and then off she goes, back down to the basement. Sarah smiles. She finds Mrs Vee charming and she would have been happy to chat to her for longer, but I'm glad the old lady's gone because I get tired of her endless talking. Mind you Sarah can talk a lot too, once she's warmed up. It's funny that Mrs Vee should assume that Sarah's my girlfriend, though perhaps not. I suppose she looks like she might be my girlfriend - more so than Lila did. And Sarah is talking now about her travels abroad, and about the injustices of the world – which is the sort of thing that gets her going and talking too much, although I'd rather have a Sarah monologue than a Mrs Vee monologue.

When the meal is ready I light a candle stuck in the top of a beer bottle and put it in the centre of the table – and it's the Rigg Beck restaurant, the best curry house in the Newlands Valley. Sarah (who is also a vegetarian) eats with gusto and gratitude - and it's nice to be cooked for, isn't it? When you live on your own and you're used to cooking the same old thing for yourself all the time, it's nice to be invited round to someone else's place for dinner. Sarah shares a flat in town with a friend, but her friend is often out and I think that Sarah does get a bit lonely. I think that loneliness of the single person is sometimes more keenly felt when you're living in town, rather than in the countryside. I say 'single person', but I'm not sure that's true of Sarah because, like I said earlier, she does have a boyfriend. But she *seems* single, and sometimes it can be a bit of a grey area... At what point does a person cease to be single and become monogamously 'hitched up'? With *marriage* I suppose. But with 'boyfriends' or 'girlfriends' or 'partners' I guess it just depends on how committed they are to each other, how committed they are to a long-term future together...

We get washed up (and the worms have already stopped coming out of the tap now) and then we go into my room, the Red Room – which is big enough for entertaining. We've got a red armchair each, but before she sits down Sarah wants to have a good nose round the room and look at my book and music collection, which is fair enough. At the window she looks out towards Cat Bells. It's getting dark now but you can still see the outline of the fell, above which there is a full moon rising. And looking down you can see the blue light flicker from Mrs Vee's TV in one of the windows. Her bedroom/sitting room is this bit of building that juts out from the main house, out from her basement kitchen. (The 'basement' here is actually ground level, because the house is built on a slope.) She watches a lot of telly or videos of old films. I'm happy to do without an 'idiot box' myself, and I think it would spoil the ambience of the Red Room. My 'home entertainment' is music or books – or, on this occasion, the company of Sarah.

And she can be quite entertaining, especially after a few drinks – and she has drunk a fair bit of lager and I can tell she's a bit tipsy. We talk about tea shop madness or whatever and it's good to get our work gripes off our chests and to have similar opinions on things. The time gets to 10.30pm and she says she'd better go, but then says she's had too much to drink and can she stay the night? 'Sure you can, Sarah. You can borrow my sleeping bag.' We take it in turns to brush our teeth (using the bottled water) at the sink, and I get my sleeping bag and mat from the top of the wardrobe and lay them on the floor. I turn out the main light and just have my bedside lamp on, and then Sarah looks away as I get undressed and get under my duvet, and then I avert my eyes as she gets undressed and climbs into the sleeping bag on the floor beside me. It occurs to me that I should've maybe offered her the bed, but she's an outdoorsy girl and no stranger to sleeping in sleeping bags on foam mats. Because my bed is really only a mattress on the floor we are both pretty much at floor level and it feels pretty cosy with her lying there alongside me. I turn off the bedside lamp and the room is still somewhat illuminated by the light of the moon – that full moon that we saw rising earlier. We chat for a while longer and then say 'goodnight', but I can't sleep - because of this moonlight, and perhaps also because of Sarah's presence. I lie there very still, and wonder if Sarah has gone to sleep yet. And then I hear her moving around, rustling the sleeping bag material, and I know she's still awake. When she stops moving I can hear an owl hooting, and the water running in the beck.

And then I hear a mouse running along the floorboards in the room. There is a big rug in the centre of the room, but around the edge it's just the bare floorboards. I've heard mice in here before and I'm not really bothered. Live and let live, they can do what they like as long as they leave me alone. I hear Sarah move in the sleeping bag. 'Sol,' she says, 'Can you hear that?' 'Yes, it's just a mouse, don't worry.' 'A *mouse*?' We both hear the scurrying feet on bare wood again, and then – more quietly – the scurrying feet on the rug. I get up on my side to take a look and I can see the mouse in the moonlight in the middle of the rug. And then I see it move towards the sleeping bag. Sarah hears it and looks toward the rug and finds herself eye to eye with the mouse – which is staring up at her. She makes a little shriek and lurches away towards my mattress. She frantically unzips the bag, gets out, stands there in just her knickers for a moment as she looks toward the mouse – which scampers away – and then she turns to the bed, pulls up the duvet and climbs in beside me. She makes a funny little frightened noise, she shivers, and she reaches out to me for a hug. And so I give her a firm protective hug and she says 'Sorry, but mice freak me out.' 'It's okay,' I say, and it feels more than okay to have her almost naked body snuggling up to me for comfort. She's quite skinny, quite *bony* in fact, but she's a woman and she's nice and warm against my body. We pull away and she says 'Can I stay here?' and of course I say 'Yes.' I rub her back affectionately. She props herself up on one elbow and I can see her bare tits – small with brown nipples, and her hairy armpits smelling quite strongly of sweat, and her face – smiling and looking different without her glasses (which she put on the bedside table). She strokes my hairy chest with little circular movements, then her hand suddenly reaches down to my pubes and brushes against my cock, before returning to my chest. She sighs deeply, and then her hand moves down again and she pulls on me gently, making me hard. And then she suddenly lies back on the mattress and says 'Come on.' I move over her to kiss her, but she says 'no kissing' and 'just do me'. And so I suck on her little tits and remove her knickers and play with her pussy and then reach for a condom in the bedside cabinet drawer, roll it on and then 'do' her, as per her request. And it feels good, but not *that* good. It's a bit weird, to be honest, to be having sex with Sarah. She reaches both hands up to the top of the mattress and her head arches back with her mouth open and I think she comes and her bushy armpits smell strong but that's okay, I find it a bit of a turn on, and then I come too, and she says 'Thanks, I needed that'. We lie there for a while, just relaxing in the warm bed lit by the moon, and I guess we are now what you might call 'fuckbuddies'.

on the treadmill

The next morning I'm in town at The Dog and Gun pub. I've just had an interview for the job of 'cook' and they've offered me the job. (Some employers prefer to use the word 'cook' rather than 'chef', which is usually an indication that you don't have to be qualified, and you will get paid less than a 'chef' for doing a cheffing job.) It wasn't much of an interview – which is typical for this sort of job. They asked me if I could cook and I said 'yes' and then they said 'when can you start?' I met the main cook, Simon, in the kitchen where he was busy making a load of mixture for steak-in-ale-pies. He's quite young and friendly and I could see from the way he was moving that he is fast – faster than I am, no doubt. There were about seven microwaves in there, which I suppose is an indication of how busy the place gets. He described himself as a 'chef de ping', which I thought was quite funny. He told me how many orders they do of a Saturday night and it sounded like an awful lot and I must admit I'm starting to get apprehensive. Will I be able to cope with doing that many? And will I be able to cope with all the meat cookery?

Now I'm in the bar having a coffee, just getting a feel for the place. I can see some black and white booklets titled *Alterlakes* stacked behind the bar next to the salted nuts, and I ask the barmaid what they are. 'Oh, that's something to do with Dave, the KP. Do you want to have a look?' And she passes one over to me and I flip through and see that it's an anthology of poems and short stories written by local people. There's a poem about the view from outside the *Caterite* supermarket, a story about some old guy fellwalking, and lots of other things. 'Dave will be in in a minute,' says the barmaid, then right on cue he walks through the door and she introduces me to him. 'Dave this is Sol, the new cook.' We shake hands, and I ask him about the *Alterlakes* booklet. It transpires that he's a writer, and he and another writer, Mark, produced the thing, and they are trying to set up a local writers' group. I say I'd be interested in joining and he suggests we could go for a pint later, hopefully with Mark too. 'Yeah great, let's do that.' I buy the booklet for £2.50, and Dave goes to work in the kitchen. And as I leave the pub I'm feeling quite positive because I've got myself a new job and it looks like I'm going to make myself some new friends – *writing* friends. I'll work a week's notice at the tea shop and then I'll be free of the place. And yet...I do feel a bit apprehensive. This new job is a step into the unknown, though I do know that it's going to be pretty full-on and I'm not really a proper chef, and maybe the disorganised amateurishness of the tea shop is more my style. I wish I didn't have to do these jobs anyway; I'd rather spend my life writing and fellrunning, but I've got to support myself somehow and I've got to stay on the treadmill. It's funny but you meet some people who are well off with inherited money or trust funds or a highly-paid partner or whatever and they don't need to work but they go out to work anyway because they'd get bored if they didn't. I suppose they feel the need to play the game of being on the treadmill and it's sociable and it gives structure and meaning to their lives and makes them feel part of society. Well if I had lots of money I certainly wouldn't go out to work in a job. I can make my own structure and meaning and I don't feel the need to be on the treadmill for any reason other than the money. But the money I can earn from being on the treadmill provides for little more than survival – rent, food, a few beers, the odd pair of fell shoes, and running a cheap second hand car if I'm lucky. It makes me think I'd rather be on the dole if I can get away with it. It's less money, but just about survivable and you get so much more free time – time that I could spend *writing*. But of course these days you're not allowed to be a 'scrounger' for long and before too long you've got to get back on that treadmill.

recreating my world

Back in town in the evening I'm on my way to meet Dave and Mark for a couple of beers and talk about this writers' group idea. I've just been to look at a room in a shared house in Wordsworth Street and we've agreed that I'll move in in a couple of weeks' time. The rent is a little more than at Rigg Beck, and the room is smaller, but it'll be handier for work and for social life and I can't face the prospect of living at Rigg Beck over the winter, especially now that I'm going to be without a car. I took it to the garage today for its MoT and it was bad news. It needs loads of work doing, including welding, and I can't afford to get it done so I'm going to have to get rid of it in a few weeks' time, when the MoT expires.

At the Skiddaw Hotel I meet Dave and Mark. Dave has fairly long hair and he has a sort of Ted Hughes look about him, although less serious-looking. He's a friendly down-to-earth Keswick lad. He's had a few different jobs in town and he plans to go down south to be a student on a creative writing degree course next year, but for the time being he's the kitchen porter at The Dog and Gun. He also says he wants to write a 'sex and catering' novel called 'KP Blue', based on his experiences working in kitchens in town – and I think this is a splendid idea, and something I've vaguely thought about doing myself. My own idea for a title is 'The Honeypot'. Mark, on the other hand, is interested in science fiction/fantasy – which holds no interest for me. He's a more middle-class professional type and he works in computers, commuting all the way to Preston, and I wonder why he chose to live in Keswick (with his wife and young child) because he's not from here and he doesn't seem to be particularly outdoorsy. Apparently he's part of some esoteric religious group but he doesn't want to talk about that much. I think he actually looks a bit like a Jehovah's Witness or something, as he's got that squeaky-clean fresh-faced conventional look about him. Anyway, he's pretty down-to-earth and he likes drinking beer so that's good. But as for sci-fi/fantasy – to me this is the very opposite of what I am trying to do and I have difficulty understanding the motivation to write such stuff. He reckons he's using it as a vehicle for his religious ideas, but I don't know why he can't do that within the context of writing about real life. Ah well, each to his own...

Anyway, we decide to meet up regularly and we decide to set ourselves a little exercise to complete before we next meet – a performance poem, which is to say a poem that is designed to be read out aloud in front of an audience. We drink more beer and we get to know each other more. I tell them about the writing I've done so far – the writing of 'Communion' and 'Only Human', both written quite quickly whilst living precariously on the dole. Dave is impressed and calls me a 'real writer', by which I think he means that I am truly committed and not just playing at it. So many would-be writers do play at it, before abandoning it in favour of focussing on the trusty old remunerative treadmill, or on some other easier 'leisure' pursuit or family life or whatever. And to make it as a writer – as someone who can produce a full-length novel – never mind getting published – does take an extraordinary amount of commitment and discipline. We talk about various forms of creative writing – poetry, short stories, songs and the novel. I have tried them all but it is the novel that interests me by far the most. Why the novel? I think because the novel offers so much scope for exploring life on so many different levels – mixing the philosophical and the religious with the mundane happenings of daily life and creating a world, or *re*creating my *own* world in my case, as my own writing is all about going back in time and revisiting the significant events, exploring them and making sense of them in an alchemical way, such that the man telling the story is no longer the one who experienced the events recorded. No matter how autobiographical a writer's intent, a certain amount of distortion or even 'fictionalisation' is unavoidable in the re-living of one's life. So it is that my writing, although 'autobiographical', is actually presented as 'fiction'. Bookshops need to categorise books one way or another and you can't just call a book 'a book'. It could be said that this book you are reading, *The Purple House*, defies categorisation, but it would be easier to simply call it a novel. And you can do what you like in a novel; it's a very open form. The very word 'novel' after all means 'new'.

After our writers' meet I drive back to Rigg Beck. There are a few people from London staying for a few days and they've moved the furniture in the kitchen to their own liking, which is annoying. They've also moved my abstract sunburst painting and left a dirty mark on it, which is even more annoying. Apparently they think the place is 'theirs' for the duration of their short stay. One of them is a cartoonist for *The Guardian*, called 'Biff', and he's friendly enough, although he was fussing about the lack of television because he wanted to watch the football. Why come to a place like Rigg Beck if that's how you want to spend your time? Mrs Vee found him an old black and white portable set and he's been ensconced with that, whilst the sun has been shining outside in a paradise for which he shows no interest. It was the same with another guy from London who came to visit the house when I was here the first time – an old painter by the name of Michael Wharton who spent all his time in his room painting these primitive 'seascapes', whilst the extraordinary natural beauty on the doorstep apparently didn't do anything for him. He would occasionally emerge into the sunshine to take tea with Mrs Vee in the garden and they would chat about London in their clipped southern middle-class voices.

And then he'd go back to his room to carry on painting these simplistic representations of endless waves in various bright colours. It looked to me like something that an infant school child would produce. And I thought to myself, why come all the way here just to do that? Anyways, back to the present...and there's a bit more noise in the house with doors banging and people up and down the stairs, and most of them aren't very friendly – because they can see (or hear) straight away that I am not one of them, a middle-class Londoner. Oh well, it could be worse, and I'll be leaving this place soon anyway.

just a quickie

In the kitchen at the tea shop I'm making some carrot and coriander soup. I know it's a bit of a cliché but it'll probably go down well with the punters because it's such a well-known combination. Beetroot and ginger would be more fun but it definitely wouldn't sell as well as carrot and coriander. I've got my onions and garlic and dried coriander frying away and making a lovely aroma – and I have to say I do love coriander, which actually goes very well with the slightly sweet taste of carrots. I've got my carrots already chopped up ready for the pan but I'll just let the onion, garlic and spice mixture cook a bit more before I put them in. Whilst I'm waiting I pop through to the dining room and grab an opened bottle of white wine from the fridge and then pour a bit of that in the pan too. Probably a waste as far as the final flavour of the soup is concerned, but I love the smell of it as the alcohol burns off. And then it's in with the chopped carrots and a kettle full of hot water, put the lid on and let it simmer away for a good while.

To tell the truth there isn't much to do this morning. Scott is on top of the washing up and I'm pretty well prepped up, apart from the mixed salad, and so I decide to go upstairs to see how Sarah's getting on. I find her in one of the guest's bedrooms, stripping off the bed linen. 'Oh hello,' she says, 'what are *you* doing here?' and laughs. 'I was bored so I thought I'd come and see you.' This is my last week at the tea shop – the last few days in fact, and I'm feeling quite laid-back, not under any pressure and not inclined to work too hard; in fact I feel like messing about a bit and having some fun. I walk over to the open window and survey the car park. It's only about half full. Well it is September now and the 'back end' of the season. I can smell my carrot and coriander soup coming out of the extractor into the cool autumnal air. Sarah comes to join me at the window and sniffs the air and says 'what've you got cooking, chef? It smells good.' She strokes my back and smiles at me. 'You can have some for your lunch, if you like,' I say. I reach down and stroke her bum through her black leggings and she goes 'Ooh...are you feeling randy?' There's a small table below the window and she leans forward and plants her hands on this whilst I fondle her buttocks. 'I'd like to visit Rigg Beck again some time before you leave,' she says. 'I enjoyed it the other night.' 'Me too,' I say, as I peel down the leggings, together with her knickers and admire her bare arse. She plants her feet a little wider apart and I stroke her between the legs, massaging her cunt. Her pubes are thick and bushy, like her armpits, and I can smell the slightly stale musky odour rising from her. I pull my hand away, spit on my fingers and resume stroking her, inserting a finger, and then another, slowly finger-fucking her. And then I break off to fumble in my pocket for my wallet, inside of which is a condom. I peel off the foil and then I unbutton my blue and white checked chef's trousers, pull down my briefs and roll the thing onto my already-hard cock. Sarah waits for me with her legs apart, her wet cunt presented to me. And so in I go, holding onto her hips as I fuck her from behind, and she goes 'Ooh that's nice...' as she holds on tightly to the edges of the table. I know she likes me to do her from behind like this because it helps to keep the experience 'impersonal' – which is what she wants. I look out over the car park and can see Paul in his chef whites, enjoying a cigarette on the balcony outside the kitchen above The Cellar Bar. And then I focus on the job in hand, which is fucking Sarah, and which I have to say is more fun than making carrot and coriander soup or chopping up a load of mixed salad. And it's all the more enjoyable for doing it in work time. Nigel could turn up at any moment and come looking for us, and I didn't lock the door behind me, but hopefully he won't - though what if he did? I'm leaving the job on Friday so I don't care. This is just a quickie anyway, and not that much different to having a smoke break. It's a 'fuck break' – that's what it is. Sarah is making these low-pitched little grunts now and her cunt is contracting round me so I let myself go and come into her, or rather into the condom. And then I pull out, peel off the condom and dispose of it carefully in the black bin liner that she's carrying round with her. She wipes a string of her own come from her inner thigh with a tissue, pulls up her knickers and leggings, gives me a peck on the cheek and says 'That was good, thankyou.' 'You're welcome Sarah, I mean thank*you*.' And then we both go back to work, Sarah to clean the rooms and me to chop up some mixed salad. My legs feel a bit unsteady as I walk back down the staircase but I'm feeling quite mellow and quite pleased with myself, naturally enough.

The soup is ready for blending now and I'll make a start on chopping that salad. And I think I'll get that bottle of white wine again and pour myself a glass and sip it slowly whilst I work. It's a bit early in the day for drinking but what the hell, I'm feeling happy and I'm feeling devil-may-care, and if Nigel comes in and sees it I'll just say it's for the cooking.

a literary event

Last night I went to a literary event at Castlegate House art gallery in Cockermouth. It was a Cumbrian author reading from his latest novel. I thought it would be worth going because, well...because I am a writer and he is a writer and it seemed like maybe an opportunity to meet some like minds and maybe make some more writing friends. But I was only there for five minutes before I felt uncomfortable in the extreme – among a lot of very cliquey middle-class people milling around, chattering and drinking glasses of wine (though I couldn't see where the wine was kept and nobody offered me any). I was conscious of these people staring at me and wondering who I was in my casual outdoorsy gear. They were all very smartly dressed and talking in posh voices and everyone seemed to know one another and I felt very out of place. And all this for *what*? The book is crap. I bought one and took it home to read and it's so lightweight, so lacking in any real substance. It's full of 'clever' turns of phrase to be sure, but the content is so shallow. And it's full of this really naff sense of humour. Were the people there last night into the book? Had they read it? I guess books like that do appeal to the polite and shallow-minded sort of reader who doesn't want to be overly challenged or faced with anything too honest and direct and real. But perhaps they were there more for the idea of being at a literary event (supposed 'high culture'), hobnobbing with the 'civilised' people. Is this what English Literature is all about? Well if it is then fuck it!

the real work

It's lunchtime now and the *mangers* are dribbling in, enticed perhaps by the smell of the carrot and coriander soup. I've got quite a few orders to do and it's surprising how that bit of wine has affected me. When you drink on the job you seem to get drunk more quickly, especially when you start so early in the day – which is unusual for me, I have to say. At The Dog and Gun Simon is allowed to drink two pints of ale every shift – and for free. It's sort of part of his wage, and I'm told I'll get the same allowance. It seems strange the employer encouraging drinking on the job and I think it's quite an old fashioned arrangement. That doesn't happen in many places nowadays. It's traditional for cheffing and drinking to go together, but you have to be careful not to drink too much too early on otherwise you lose your speed and your co-ordination and everything might go tits up. Not that there's any danger of things going tits up this afternoon...I've only had one glass so far and it's not going to be busy, and the new chef Drew will be in at about 3pm to start preparing dishes for the evening menu. Drew is okay. He's good at his job, but like a lot of chefs he's quite full of himself and arrogant and he seems to think he's in charge round here, even though he's only been here a couple of weeks. And, to be honest, I find him quite a dull person. There's not a great deal of conversation, not much of a crack. And really, being able to have a crack with your colleagues is what makes a kitchen job bearable, or indeed *any* job bearable – unless of course you happen to be working on your own.

I pour another glass of wine and reflect that this aint too bad really; it could be a lot worse. I could be labouring on a building site (which I have done in the past), or I could be having to stand to attention all day long in an outdoor shop (which I have also done), pouncing on customers as soon as they walk through the door and giving them the full technical spiel on the latest pair of walking trousers and addressing them as 'sir' or 'madam', and then at the till making sure that they are on the customer database so that the company can bombard them with catalogues, and then finally wishing them a phoney 'Have a nice day!'. Christ no, I don't want to have to do that again, although I may have to at some point, you never know, you've got to be flexible and be prepared to turn your hand to whatever is available if you want to survive round here. It's basically a choice of catering or retail, or maybe labouring – and at the same time I've got to somehow find a way to keep the writing work going as well. That's the *real* work.

PART THREE

make soup, not war

Lying in bed now it's early in the morning and very quiet. I feel slight vibrations but can't be sure where they are coming from. Maybe it's Mrs Vee moving around in the basement, or maybe it's the house moving slightly in the wind. I kept waking in the night to strange creaking noises in the house, caused no doubt by the wild windy weather and the house gently swaying. One of these days this house is going to collapse. In fact it might fall down at any moment, but it's a risk I'm prepared to take. I also had a disturbing dream last night, though I can't quite remember how it went. It was to do with this place, though it was somehow different. Mrs Vee was selling up. This house has recurred in dreams when I've not been living here. Obviously it's a special place for me, a place that means something to me.

As I lie in bed my nose and my toes feel cold. I'm wearing a fleece hat, full body thermal underwear and thick woollen socks, but I'm still cold. It's early April but we've had some quite wintry weather with snow on the ground and these cold northerly winds that blow straight through the rickety house. Again those vibrations. And now I'm thinking that it's maybe the movement of my own heart beating that's the cause of it. Every time my heart beats my whole body very gently shudders. But what's *that*? – a loud *thud* and it's definitely the building that shudders. And now I hear the scrape of wooden furniture on a wooden floor, and it's Ray getting up and moving around in the room next door. I glance at my alarm clock and it's 6am. And then I hear Radio 2 coming through the wall very loud and bassy from those big old speakers – and the spell of tranquillity is broken. *Shit!* I get dressed and go round to his room to complain.

Although the door is closed, one of the wooden panels has been smashed in and I can see him pacing up and down and muttering to himself. I call out his name 'Ray', and 'Can I have a word?' He says 'Come in' and so in I go, into the Red Room that was once 'mine'. I ask him to turn down the radio, tell him that it's disturbing me, and ask him to please be more considerate. He goes on the defensive. 'What's wrong with listening to the radio?' he says, and then he starts a ranting monologue, not listening to what I have to say (going on, ironically, about how nobody listens to anybody else these days), and he makes me angry and we end up shouting at each other and it gets to the stage of me prodding him in the chest and threatening to hit him. And then he says 'Tell me when I can get up in the morning. You're the zoo-keeper and I'm in the cage.' And I feel a bit sorry for him. He is intelligent, and most of the time reasonable, and perhaps I am being *un*reasonable in asking him to quieten down his music. He's got to live. And what *is* living for him? Pacing up and down his 'cage', listening to the radio, or maybe a Krishnamurti tape. Sometimes he scrawls on the walls things like 'MAKE SOUP, NOT WAR' (and he seems to live off tinned soup). He's written on his old khaki canvas shoulder bag too – the way schoolchildren do. Sometimes he goes out for walks, but he doesn't seem to have any friends. The other day he went for a walk and locked himself out of his room. On his return he got back in by smashing the wooden panel in the door with an axe. No doubt it would have been easier to go and see his mother, Mrs Vee, for a spare key, but they've fallen out already and they aren't speaking. I feel sorry for the guy, but at the same time he's doing my head in.

And what is 'living' for me? Working on my writing, working at my job at the Swinside Inn, going out running, and being with friends. I feel like I'm not spending enough time with friends. Oh well, tonight I'm going into town to meet my old friend Max. He's thinking of coming to join me here at the house. But perhaps I should explain to you what I am doing here again anyway... The year is 2000 and I have come here to work on my third novel, 'Black Sail', the first draft of which I wrote over the winter, whilst unemployed and living in a shared house in Windermere. I had to leave the house in Windermere as the landlord was selling up. I had quite a productive time there, getting the first draft of Black Sail handwritten and then typed up. But it's only a first draft and it still needs a lot of work and I needed to find somewhere suitable to live to carry on working on it. I got in touch with Mrs Vee and arranged to visit her to discuss the possibility of moving back to the house. She told me she'd had just one tenant – in the flat – who'd been there for a couple of years, but who'd left suddenly a few months ago. The flat was in a really bad state, with rubbish everywhere, broken furniture, a couple of broken windows, and a big hole in the ceiling of the 'living room', where the rain came in. She said I could live here rent-free for a few weeks in return for tidying the place up, painting the walls and arranging for the building repair work – and then it would be just a low rent of about £40 a week. It was a rather vague arrangement, but it seemed like a good opportunity to me, especially since I didn't have any money, or anywhere else to go. Living in the flat I'd have plenty of space, and with two bedrooms I could maybe get a friend to help me pay the rent, once I'd started paying. I also managed to get myself a part-time job of kitchen assistant at the Swinside Inn. It could have been full-time, but I opted for 30 hours a week because I wanted as much time as possible to work on my writing, and I figured I should be able to manage – with no rent, or a *low* rent.

It's been about two weeks now since I moved in, and I have to say it's turning out to be a bit of a nightmare. There was no electricity at first – something to do with the electricity meter having been tampered with by the previous tenant, apparently. Anyway the electricity company have been and fixed that now. Also there is no water coming through to the bathroom, so that I have to use the communal bathroom on the landing, which isn't really a problem as there's only me and Ray using it, but the plumbing does need fixing. I contacted a couple of local plumbers, but when I said I was at Rigg Beck they said they weren't interested. No doubt Mrs Vee has a bad reputation hereabouts as a bad payer, or as being 'difficult to work with' – as one of the plumbers put it. And of course she *is* difficult. She's more difficult than she used to be – more senile I suppose, and possibly even more smelly. She's always coming to talk to me in her endless monologues. Yesterday she came up and knocked on the door, but didn't wait before barging in and plonking herself down on a chair and filling the air with the stench of stale piss, talking and talking and talking. And I said 'I'm sorry but I don't have time to listen to you,' but she just kept on and on. I've only been here two weeks and she's demanding rent – not the £40 a week that we originally agreed, but £80, which she now reckons it's worth. I've spent quite a lot of time cleaning and tidying the place. I've bought some paint, but I haven't started painting yet. She wants me to paint the living room but I can't see the point when there's a bloody great hole in the roof where the rain comes in. She needs to get the house re-roofed but she can't afford to do that, so she thinks that if I do a bit of painting it'll be okay. Is she mad? Yes, she is, and so is her son 'Ray'. And perhaps I'm mad too for coming here.

What at first seemed to be a good idea has gone disastrously wrong. I wanted a room to write. I cannot think of a *worse* place to write now that I am here. I can't relax here, can't get a good night's sleep, and consequently I can't concentrate on my writing. I've wasted money buying bits and pieces to improve the flat, and now the mad witch is demanding way too much rent. She should consider herself lucky she's got someone to live here at all. Most people would consider it unfit for human habitation. I'm going to have to leave or get someone else in to share the rent. Max says he's interested as he's unhappy with his noisy shared house in town, and wants more space to do his painting. He's thinking he could use the 'living room' as studio space. Anyway, he's going to come up and see the place tomorrow.

unfit for human habitation

I leave Ray in his 'cage' and go through to the kitchen in the flat to get some breakfast: a banana, a bowl of muesli with soya milk, and a black coffee. I get the water for the kettle from the tap - and the water is flowing again, which it wasn't yesterday. Yesterday there was no water coming out of any taps in the house and so Ray and I took a walk up the beck to investigate the problem. On the fellside there was a dam of rubble that had obstructed and diverted the stream away from its usual course to the collecting tank down below. I spent some time digging this out and deepening the stream channel to improve the flow of water. Ray just stood there, prattling on like his mother and saying 'I can't help, I've got a bad back.' 'Ray' is not his real name, and when he arrived the other day he introduced himself as 'Peter Simple', but now he wishes to be called 'Ray'. I know that his real name is Adam Vergauwen, but he is free to call himself what he likes. My own name, Sol is not my 'real' name, but one I chose for myself. It is in fact an old school nickname that relates to my original surname, which I also changed. And Ray's mother, Mrs Vee changed her name too. And this self-naming and self-creating, together with a blurring of fact and fiction, seems to go with the territory of the Purple House.

I look around this kitchen, whilst I'm waiting for the kettle to boil. I like the way it's been painted bright pink and green – as bright as *Post-it* stickers. It took me a long time to clean this kitchen, but I think it's the best room in the flat. There's an old electric cooker, a fridge and lots of wooden shelves and cupboards which are painted in the punky pink and green. I walk over to the window by the sink, where I've put up a bamboo blind. I don't like being stared at by passers-by who stop in their cars to gawp at the house like it's some kind of tourist attraction. 'Look, there's someone in there – standing at the window...Oh my god, somebody actually *lives* in that place!' At the same time I want to let some light in and see the world outside – the trees beside the road, the fellside rising up and the blue sky. I pull the cord at the side of the blind but only one side of the blind rolls upwards. It should be such a simple thing but I can't get both sides of the blind to roll up together, so I leave it for now, partly rolled up at an annoyingly lopsided angle, and make my coffee and sit down on a wooden stool to eat my bowl of muesli.

It's cold in here – so cold that I can see the steam of my breath. I've got to go to work at the Swinny today, but I only start at eleven o' clock so I've got time to do some work on my writing and also go for a quick run. I've got the first draft of 'Black Sail' typed up but I'm not entirely happy with it. There is one problematical chapter in particular that needs quite a bit of work – editing or re-writing or maybe even ditching – but I want to go through the whole book again, typing up a second draft on my electric typewriter – a draft that will hopefully be to my satisfaction, and therefore 'final'. It's quite a big job and it'll take me at least a few months, if all goes well – but things are *not* going well, distracted as I am by the issues of living in this house.

There's a knock on the door. *Shit*. 'Helloo...Sol' calls out Mrs Vee in her high-pitched pleading voice. She knocks again, using the old brass door knocker (which originally came from Durham Cathedral, so someone told me), the scary demonic face – like a gargoyle. I freeze and wait for her to go away. I hear the door handle turn but the door won't open because I've locked it. There's a pause and I can hear her heavy breathing, and I can almost smell her from here. Her footsteps shuffle away and I hear her knocking on Ray's door. 'Adam,' she calls out. I can imagine her peering in through the broken door panel, and there's nowhere for the poor guy to hide. I hear his footsteps on the bare boards, and the door opening and some conversation. I can't hear what they are saying but the voices get louder as it develops into an argument and I hear Mrs Vee say the word 'doctor', and 'you can't stay here.'

I take my coffee into my bedroom-cum-writing room – the 'Yellow Room', and sit down at my desk and open the black lever arch file containing the typescript of 'Black Sail'. It's going to be hard to concentrate with the sound of Mrs Vee and her son arguing next door, and the threat of her coming to knock on my door again, besides which it's so *cold* in here. I've got this oil-filled radiator on, but it's not radiating much heat – not enough to warm this room anyway. I put my woolly hat on and start reading the typescript, pencilling in notes and crossing out bits of text here and there. Apart from the coldness I'm quite pleased with this Yellow Room, which is the best room in the flat, and which is where I've set up 'home'. It's the cleanest and least damp room, with lemon yellow walls and a window overlooking the copse and the bend in the road. It's got a single bed, some shelves, a round dining table, and my writing desk and chair. I was going to put the desk below the window, but realised I'd be on show to every passing car or pedestrian so I've put it against the wall instead, so that there are no visual distractions – just a blank yellow wall. The wall is lit by my desk lamp, which is perched on top of a cardboard box and aimed at the wall rather than the desk to give just the right level of diffuse light. But I can't concentrate...I can hear Mrs Vee and 'Ray' arguing next door. My hands are cold as I make a pencil annotation on the typescript and my handwriting is not fluid. It's blowing a gale outside and a draught is coming through the ill-fitting sash window frame and it's uncomfortably cold in here – too cold to write. I'm determined to get on with the writing work, but sometimes there are just too many distractions and the mind can't focus and it's better to leave it alone and do something else. I close the Black Sail file and start making a list of things that are wrong with the house, a list that I intend to present to Mrs Vee at some point as evidence that the flat is not worth the amount of rent she is asking: *1) Toilet doesn't work – plumbing needs fixing. 2) Water leaking in through ceiling of living room at various points, and the whole room v. damp and mouldy. 3) Unlikelihood of repairs being carried out to the roof to prevent ingress of water. 4) Broken window in living room; window boarded up in front bedroom; some other windows sealed shut or need repairs to sash mechanism. 5) Lack of interest by local tradesmen in carrying out work at Rigg Beck because Mrs Vee has a bad reputation as a non-payer, or just being very difficult to work with. 6) The fire alarm system isn't working. 7) As far as letting rooms is concerned the house is probably officially condemned or condemnable as being unfit for human habitation...* There is a sudden strong gust of wind and I can feel the house swaying and hear it creaking. I add another point: *8) The house might fall down at any moment.*

I get up from my chair and look around the room. I've tried to make it my 'own'. I am trying to make a 'home' out of the flat – which is a natural instinct I suppose, but also ridiculous considering what this place is like, and what my lifestyle is like. Wherever I go (and I have had so many addresses) I try to make a home of the place. Most importantly I need a writing desk or table. I need some shelves for my files and books, and for my stereo and my CDs and tapes. I need somewhere to put my clothes and my running shoes. I also need a bed of course, and – since the

Yellow Room didn't actually have one - I brought the one I'd slept in at the house in Windermere. It was going to get thrown out as the landlord had sold the house, which was going to be completely refurbished by the new owners. Incredibly I managed to transport it in the back of my car (I now have another Mk 1 VW Golf – a green one this time), in two stages – first the base and then the mattress, with it sticking right out the back of the rear door and secured by just a bungee cord. Anyway, I have too much stuff to live the life of a vagabond. Really I should try and get my possessions down to just one car load at the very most. But of course one accumulates things, and they are useful... I've got all my clothes and some other bits and pieces stored in the front bedroom – where there is a large wardrobe. I walk through to that room now to get some running kit, because I'm going to go for a run. I'm hoping to sublet this bedroom – possibly to Max, if he's interested, to make living here more viable. It's a bigger room than the Yellow Room and it's got a double bed and more furniture. On the downside the front window is boarded up and the floor has a disconcerting slope to it. If you place a ball on the floor at the door end of the room you can watch it roll, picking up momentum as it rolls down the slope to the outside wall of the house. Some building work was done a few years ago to shore up this side of the house. A great big concrete block was laid at the foot of the house, and someone spray-painted their name and 'R.I.P' in large letters on the concrete. A guy at the Swinny told me it was the name of the builder who had laid the block, and then not been paid by Mrs Vee for his work. Anyway, the floor slopes quite badly, and I imagine that if the house does collapse it will be this side that's the first to go. The room is a bit damp and has a musty smell to it. It doesn't help that there are no windows that will open in here. The other day I cut a small ventilation window in the board where the front window used to be, which looks a bit mad, but at least it lets some air in.

Anyways, it's time to get out for a run, which will hopefully put me in a more positive frame of mind before I go to work at the Swinny. I put on some tights and a thermal top, a windproof jacket, a different hat, gloves and my road shoes – because I haven't got a lot of time and so I'm just going to have a trot round the lanes. And then I sneak out the flat door (although Mrs Vee has left Ray alone now and is probably back in her basement), down the stairs and out the front door. And I set off jogging down the road, a bit sluggish at first, then getting into my stride and enjoying the cold wind against my face, past the turn off for Stair and on towards Braithwaite, turning off just before the village, doubling back at first on a lane that takes me below the forested lump of Swinside to the inn of the same name, then down to Stair and back up to the house, where I have a quick bath, change into my work clothes and jump in the car and drive to work – back up the road to the Swinny.

coming through

Striding into the kitchen, I see the clock on the wall says that it's five minutes past eleven (and I start work at 11am). I glance at my wristwatch, which says 11.02am, and say 'Good Morning, Billy!' Billy the chef is at the stove, stirring something in a huge aluminium pan – which is belching steam and a strong unpleasant meaty smell. He turns to me and his thick spectacles are all steamed up. There's a dramatic pause as he stares at me for a moment through those steamed-up glasses, and I wonder if he can see me at all. He's a short fat bald and ugly Scotsman who is half-blind and usually bad-tempered. 'Good *afternoon*!' he bawls aggressively. I grab an apron and think to myself – oh no, not another shift with that loud arrogant smart-arsed tosser. 'What shall I do?' I ask him. 'You can get here on time for starters,' he says, then there is another pause as he stirs whatever it is he's got in that pan. 'What's in there?' I say. 'Stock,' he says. I walk up to his side and look in the pan and there's a load of chicken bones and fragments of meat in a greasy horrible stinking liquid. (I'm a vegan now, by the way.) I sense that he doesn't like me standing next to him, too close to his personal space. He's the boss of the kitchen and I'm his assistant and he wants to keep a bit of distance between us. 'You can do that washing up and then wash the lettuce and get the salad stuff together.' 'Okay,' I say, and set to work – putting the last of the breakfast crockery through the dishwasher and scrubbing the pans that he's used this morning. And then I give the sink a good clean, fill it with cold water and throw in the fancy lettuces – oak leaf, lollo rosso and radicchio (which seem to be used by every single pub and restaurant in the Lake District).

With the oak leaves and the lollo rossos I just twist the stalk off the bottom and the leaves all come away and fall into the water. But with the radicchio I have to use a knife at the base to separate the tightly packed leaves. This lettuce is an attractive purple colour, but it tastes very bitter so I can't see the point myself. Anyway I fill the sink with two each of these lettuces and give them a good swish around. 'Put some salt in,' says Billy. 'It kills the bugs.' Quite often there are creepy crawlies hiding amongst the leaves, and they float to the surface, some of them still alive – although maybe the salt will kill them if I leave them to soak for a while.

Next I get a chopping board, and with a good sharp knife I start slicing up the cucumber, tomato, mixed pepper and red onion – which will be used for garnishes, sandwiches and main dishes with salad. Leanne, the Australian waitress/barmaid breezes into the kitchen with a 'G'day' and a broad smile. Thank god there are people like her working in this place to shine a bit of light into the kitchen. She helps herself to some strips of pepper and munches away. Billy sees her and bawls 'No grazing in the kitchen!' She looks at me with an amused downward smile, says 'Sorry, chef' and then walks back out into the bar to roll the cutlery in paper napkins.

'Go and get me some onions and a big tin of tomatoes from the dry store,' barks Billy. So off I go, out the kitchen to an outhouse on the roadside – which is where we keep all the tinned and dry stuff, as well as some of the veg. It's nice just to get out of the kitchen for a few minutes and breathe in some cool fresh air and see what the weather's doing. The wind has dropped a bit but it's still a cold day – cold, dry and clear, though a bit dull. There's some snow on the fell tops, and it's a good view from here of Barrow and Causey Pike. The beer garden here is a great place to sit and drink on a summer's day. Roll on summer...

Back in the kitchen Billy starts making some tomato soup, the quick and easy tomato soup that you get everywhere – some fried onion and garlic, a big tin of tomatoes, a bit of dried basil, and some salt, pepper and sugar, and hey presto, you've got 'Tomato and Basil Soup, £2.95' (this is the year 2000). The crusty rolls served with the soup are called 'rustic rolls' and are bought in frozen and part-cooked from a big catering company that delivers once a week. We bang them in the oven to finish cooking them and make them crusty, but inside they are usually still a bit doughy, and personally I think they are crap, but this is what so many pubs and cafes and restaurants use – the mass-produced cardboard roll served with the tinned tomato soup. Bon appétit!

Lunchtime comes round and Leanne comes in with some checks for soup and sandwiches and fish and chips. It's my job to make sandwiches, which is easy enough, and a bit of a come-down really when I've been used to being the main man in the kitchen – but hey, I'm not complaining, my main job is *writing* (not that I've been doing much of that lately), and it suits me if the 'day job' is easy. For the soup I have to just warm a couple of rolls (that we cooked off earlier) in the oven and then ladle the soup into the bowls from the pan on the stove. As I walk up to the stove with the bowls Billy walks to the stove from the other side with a big aluminium tray of chips that he's just fried. He's got his head down and doesn't see me until the last moment, nearly bumping into me with the tray of chips. 'Watch out!' he bawls. 'Always tell me you are there!' he shouts. I don't want an accident any more than he does, but he wasn't watching where he was going, and even if he was, his vision is so poor that he might not have seen me anyway. I say 'Yes, boss,' and in future I will try to always remember to announce my presence with 'I'm coming through' or some such. I ladle the soup into the bowls, place the bowls on plates with the 'rustic rolls' and ring a bell to summon Leanne.

And so it goes, the lunchtime shift – soups, sandwiches, fish and chips, a steak in ale pie and a couple of 'Lamb Henrys'. It's been quite a quiet one, to be honest. I get washed up and I'm away at 3pm. Some days I do the evening shift as well, but today that's it for the day and I am now free to do my own thing. I'm going to meet Max in town for a beer at 5.30pm, and then we're going to go round to a youth hostel staff house where we'll meet up with some friends and I'm supposed to be cooking them all a meal. I've got a couple of hours to kill before I go into town, so I'll go back to the house and maybe do some work on the flat, or maybe even do some work on my book. I've done hardly any work on 'Black Sail' since I moved in, and I really want to get on with it, but at the same time I feel I'm under a bit of pressure to 'refurbish' the flat. I've bought some paint but painting seems pointless when there are major problems (such as the hole in the roof) and, to coin an expression, it would be 'like polishing a turd'.

the bohemian nature

Sitting at a table by the fire in The George Hotel, Max and I each have a pint of Jennings Bitter and we've got some catching up to do. Since that season I was at Black Sail and he was at Buttermere Youth Hostel he went to Edinburgh for the winter to work in a bookshop, then returned to Keswick last spring to work for the YHA for a season, and then he went back to his home town of Bradford for the winter, and now he's back in Keswick and working at the Tourist Information Centre and lodging in a flat just a bit further up the street from this pub – above The Red Fort curry house in fact. 'And how's it going, old marra?' I ask him. The job seems like quite a good number to me, and Max has to admit that it's okay as jobs go but it still annoys and frustrates him and it seems he's not really suited to working with the general public, even though that's what he always ends up doing. He's not really a 'people person' or, to put it another way, he doesn't like people. He appreciates his few close friends, but he doesn't seem to get any satisfaction out of advising and helping the tourists and customers he is employed to serve. His communication skills are good and there's no doubt that he can do the job adequately – it's just that he hates it, just as he's hated just about every job he's ever done. What the answer is I don't know, and probably there isn't one. At least he's in the Lakes and Keswick is a good place to live, with fells on the doorstep and friends at hand too. He showed me round his digs before we came here and he's got a nice gaff, sharing quite a smart and reasonably-priced 2nd floor flat with a young 'professional' woman who he gets on with fine. It's just the noise from the street, and the noise from the building work on the floor below. And I must admit, that would annoy me too. Like Max, I am sensitive to noise – and perhaps even more so. Having lived in some really quiet places such as Black Sail and now Rigg Beck I would find it hard to live in town with all the road traffic noise. And this is only a *small* town. As for building work – hammering and drilling and general banging around, well nobody wants to live with that going on around you (quite often into the evening says Max) and it would drive me mad, and is driving Max mad, which is why he's thinking of coming up to Rigg Beck to share the flat with me. He's going to come up tomorrow, on a day off, to have a look at the front bedroom. I've warned him that it's a bit dilapidated, but that hasn't put him off. He's attracted by the quietness of the location, the plentiful space, and the distance (geographic and psychic) from Main Street. He's attracted to the bohemian nature of the place, and he's thinking it could be good for his art work, and I've told him he could use the 'living room' as a studio.

He did quite a bit of painting last winter, whilst he was unemployed and living at home – so much so that he recently had an exhibition of his abstract landscapes at Keswick Museum. But he's not been doing a lot lately, what with working full-time at the TIC and lodging in a flat where there isn't much space to do it. Your average flat or house is set up so that you've got a bedroom for sleeping and a 'living room' for watching TV (not that watching telly is really 'living') and there aint much space to do much else. Most of the floor-space in Max's bedroom, as in so many bedrooms, is taken up by a double bed – not that he needs a double, and it would suit him better if it was a single bed to make room for some painting-space or desk-space, but it's not his flat and it's not his furniture so he has to make do with a situation that is far from ideal, a situation that is restricting and frustrating his creative drive. It's a situation with which I am familiar myself. When I've been to look at rooms to rent my first question is 'Will I be able to get a desk in there?' The trouble is that in most houses bedrooms are set up for sleeping and getting dressed and not much else (except perhaps some more TV-watching). Certainly they are not set up for artistic or creative endeavours. Such endeavours are on the margins of society and not catered for by the treadmill mindset of get up, go to work, come back, have a meal and watch TV. He or she who needs some solitude and some peace and quiet and space to practice painting or writing or just thinking is forced into an outhouse or a purple house with a hole in the roof and a mad landlady (unless of course you are lucky enough to have the money to buy or rent more than just a little box-of-bricks prison – but of course the artistic impulse/temperament tends to run counter to the careering, money-making mentality that might make this possible). So what can you do? 'Have another pint of Jennings mate, and come and live with me at the Purple House.' 'Well you know I might just do that, but I need to have a look at the place tomorrow.'

And so we have another pint of Jennings Bitter – which is one of my favourites, as it happens. Dark brown and smooth and quite strong-flavoured (though not strong in alcohol) it slips down nicely and hits the spot just right. And the pub is one of my favourites, if not *the* favourite of the pubs in town – olde worlde and cosy, with some interesting old pictures on the walls (including a photograph of the Skiddaw hermit with a big bushy beard) and with a fire burning, and popular with both locals and visitors. We're sitting at a table in the room on the right as you go in, where there is also a group of four middle-aged fellwalkers – two couples enjoying a post-walk refresher before they go back to their B and Bs or their hotel and get changed and go out for dinner. And Max and I will be having dinner in a little while – a meal cooked by myself at the YHA staff house on Ratcliffe Place, and shared with some youth hostel friends – when they get back from doing their evening shift. We've got a bit of time yet, and so we talk about fellrunning. 'I'd like to do Ennerdale this year,' I say. I did it three years ago and had a good run, clocking 4 hours 30 minutes and coming in 10th, just ahead of Jos Naylor. I felt bad about beating him because I'd run with him all the way from Haycock to just before Crag Fell (he showing me all the best lines), whereupon I pulled away for the last couple of miles – but a race is a race is a race, and you have to push yourself to do your best, and I guess I had a bit more left in me than he did at the end. Oh well, he was sixty years old by then, to my thirty-three. I was grateful to him for showing me the way, and honoured to be in his company. To tell the truth I haven't been doing anywhere near enough training to be seriously contemplating doing the race this year, but I can dream, and you never know...' I think I'm finished with racing,' says Max. 'It's an ego-driven thing which I've grown out of. I don't need to do it anymore, and I'm happy to just go for long runs on my own.' His statement sounds plausible, and I must admit that the long solitary fell run is probably the most important kind of run for me. Also I do sometimes find the battling of 'egos' and all the talk about times and positions a bit tedious, but on the other hand racing is sociable and by not racing he'll be missing out on 'the crack'. To be honest I don't think he appreciates the crack as much as some, and not as much as myself. He describes himself as an 'isolationist', and part of his nature rejoices in isolation, but he is only human and he knows that 'no man is an island' and that he needs a certain amount of social life. Talking of which, it's time to leave the George and head for Ratcliffe Place...

our little dinner party

It's just a few minutes' walk up St. John's Street and then down Church Street to Ratcliffe Place. I knock on the door, which is opened by a girl called Jess – long wavy blonde hair, a nose-stud, a smile, a grey marl hoody, jeans and bare feet. She's quite short, and of a 'chunky' build (though don't tell her I said that). 'Now then!' I say. 'Now *then*!' she replies, and laughs. She lets us in and we go through to the kitchen and she shows me where everything is, including quite a good selection of fresh veg. I put on an old plastic apron and set to work with a sharp knife, slicing up onions and peppers and courgettes and mushrooms, whilst Max and Jess sit in the lounge and watch telly (the back end of the Channel Four News). I hear Jess try to strike up a conversation with Max, but these two don't know each other very well and I sense that it's a bit awkward. There's a radio in the kitchen and so I switch it on. I've got to have tunes when I'm cooking. And coming over the airwaves it's The Manic Street Preachers and *The Masses Against The Classes* - which is a fine tune. There's a bag of penne pasta and I measure it out into a pan and put the kettle on to boil. We're going to have a veggie pasta dish, which should suit everyone. Jess and Bea are veggies and Max and Jaz are not fussy. Jaz and Bea work at the 'Derwentwater' youth hostel just a couple of miles down the Borrowdale road and they'll be cycling here when they finish their evening shift (which shouldn't be too long, this being a Monday). Jaz lives at the hostel, but Bea lives in this house with a few other assistant wardens that work at the Keswick hostel, including Jess, and a couple of recently-recruited lads who won't be part of our little dinner party.

At 8.30pm the back door opens and it's Bea and Jaz. 'Something smells good,' says Bea with a broad smile, as she strides into the kitchen. Then Jaz follows behind in his fluorescent yellow cycling jacket, a slightly awkward half-smile on his unshaven face, his large nose twitching, his eyes blinking and his movements slow and uncertain as he removes his jacket in the doorway. 'Did you have many in tonight?' I inquire of them. 'No, not many,' says Bea, and she opens a cupboard and produces a bottle of red wine. 'Would you like a glass?' 'Yes,' I say, and so she opens the bottle and pours me one, and then announces that she's going to have a shower and disappears upstairs. Jaz helps himself to a glass of wine and goes through to the lounge with the bottle to join Max and Jess. My pasta dish is almost complete now. I transferred it from the pan into a tray, sprinkled it with breadcrumbs, and now it's baking in the oven. I've grated some cheese separately into a bowl so that people can add that to their portion, if they so wish, and I've also made a bowl of lettuce and tomato salad. I clear down the work surface and get some cutlery and take it through to the lounge, where there's a large dining table. And then I grab my glass of wine and join Max, Jess and Jaz. Max and Jaz have known each other a long time, and they are having a good old chinwag, whilst Jess watches TV with her 'John Lennon glasses' on.

By and by Bea comes down, refreshed from her shower and wearing a navy blue check shirt and baggy jeans – and looking very attractive I think. She's of medium height, in her early twenties, of buxom build, with shoulder-length dark brown hair and big soulful brown eyes. She pours herself a glass of wine, by which time there's none left, but 'Don't worry,' says Jaz, and he goes into the kitchen and produces another bottle from his black canvas pannier bag. I go through to the kitchen too to portion out the pasta bake onto the dinner plates. Bea comes to help me carry the plates through to the lounge, and then we all sit down to eat and drink wine and talk about what we've been up to job-wise and outdoors-wise and other-wise.

I've known Max for years, through the YHA; likewise Jaz. I've known Bea and Jess just the last couple of years, through the YHA connection (though I haven't worked for the YHA myself for a year or so). We've all moved around a lot, living and working in different places, but Keswick seems to have drawn us back like a magnet, and so here we are – a bunch of youngish single transient unsettled outdoorsy types, based in Keswick for the time being... When I say 'youngish' Max, Jaz and myself are actually in our mid to late thirties and therefore fast approaching middle age. The girls on the other hand are both in their early twenties and therefore definitely young. Bea is not long out of university (she's an English graduate) and she still has quite a student air about her. Jess hasn't been to uni, but she's dabbled at all kinds of different courses – from holistic massage to organic horticulture, in between working seasons for the YHA, often as a 'relief warden' (as she is now), which involves much travelling around, working at different hostels in the whole of the 'Northern Region', and sometimes further afield – a very unsettled way of life, but it seems to suit her. I've moved round quite a bit myself, doing different jobs in different places, and so has Max, but Jaz has worked almost entirely at the Derwentwater youth hostel for the last ten years. He usually has a (seasonal) girlfriend recruited from the hostellers but I don't think he's got anyone at the moment and so he's 'in between girlfriends' and therefore more available to his male friends and more inclined to throw himself into fellrunning. I suggest that he, Max and myself could meet up for a fell run at a mutually convenient time – which will probably have to be when our days off coincide, and therefore probably difficult to arrange.

Bea is interested to hear all about the Purple House and says she wants to come up some time, and even says she'll help me with the decorating. And Jess wants to come and have a look too, and so we arrange for them to come up and visit me the day after tomorrow. Jess says she's looking for somewhere to live because she's going to stop working for the YHA soon and she's going to be working for the newish veggie cafe in town, (where I worked myself for a while last year).

At about ten-thirty the young lads from Keswick hostel appear and they want to watch a video in the lounge and smoke some dope, and it seems like our little dinner party is coming to a close. We finish off the wine and take the plates through to the kitchen to wash up, and pretty soon Max and Jaz declare that they are off home to bed. I'm fairly tired myself though I wouldn't have minded extending the evening a bit. After Max and Jaz have gone I find myself chatting to Bea in the backyard, in the dark. She asks me how 'Black Sail' is coming along and says she'd like to read some of it. She also says she wants to do some writing herself, and so I suggest we meet up one afternoon to talk about writing and maybe do a little writing exercise together. 'Yeah great,' she says. 'We could meet in the George over a drink. How about this Thursday afternoon?' 'Cool. Let's do it!' Finally we say 'goodnight' and we have a hug and I kiss her on the cheek. We half pull away and there's a lingering moment of us looking at each other, still holding on to each other, when it seems we might kiss each other on the lips...but the moment passes and we pull away and I say 'See you on Thursday. The George at 3 o' clock.'

what a madhouse!

On arrival back at Rigg Beck I get out the car and see the blue light flicker of Mrs Vee's TV in a basement window. I open the big old front door and close it gently behind me. In the hallway I get a whiff of stale piss, which suggests the old lady has walked through here recently. I creep up the stairs, not wanting to cause any vibration that will announce my presence (this despite the revving of my car and the crunching and grinding of gears – for the clutch is knackered – less than a minute previously, which surely did announce my return). She's not likely to come upstairs now, but you never know.

As I climb the stairs I hear voices coming from Ray's room. When I get to the landing I stop to listen.

It sounds like he's got somebody in there and they're having a conversation – an *argument* in fact. There's a gruff and aggressive voice, and also a higher-pitched whining voice, which sounds like Ray (Adam). I go up to his door and peer in through the smashed-in panel and I can see him sat up in bed, the only person in the room, having an argument with himself in two separate voices. The deep voice doesn't seem to belong to him, and yet it's coming out of his mouth, admonishing himself over something. It's like he's possessed, though I guess he would be diagnosed as 'schizophrenic'. I call out to him 'Ray, are you okay?' and he just shouts back 'Go away!' I look at the wall near the door and can see some fresh scrawling, including 'THE LADY DOTH PROTEST TOO MUCH'. I leave him alone and unlock the door to 'my' flat. It's freezing cold in here, as usual. I get myself a whisky nightcap, switch on the oil-filled radiator in the Yellow Room, and sit down on the bed to read a bit of Nietzsche's *Zarathustra* – but I can't relax because I can hear Ray/Adam ranting and raving next door. What a madhouse! And I want to live in a normal house with sane people. No matter how self-contained or strong or determined I am there's no escaping the bad energy that's in this house these days.

the 'living' room

The next day sees me doing another lunchtime shift at The Swinny, and then waiting back at the house for Max to come and have a look. He arrives at 3pm with Jaz, the pair of them on bikes, and they both have a good look round the flat. I show Max the front bedroom with the sloping floor and the boarded-up window with the ventilation hole. 'How much would the rent be?' he asks, to which I don't have a definite answer. 'I reckon that we offer her £60 a week for the flat, so that's £30 a week each.' £60 is more than I'm paying at the moment, or more than I'm supposed to be paying on my own. The truth is that I've been here three weeks and I haven't paid her any rent yet, although I intend to start paying her £40 a week (as agreed) fairly soon. I leave Max in the front bedroom on his own to give him time to ponder over it, and then I join Jaz, who is walking slowly and fascinatedly round the 'living room'. There's a roll of filthy damp carpet on the floor which needs throwing out, but which is too heavy and awkward for me to remove myself, so I ask Jaz to help me carry it downstairs. There's a pause, and I can see he's reluctant to help. He probably doesn't want to get his hands dirty, but he can hardly say no, and so he bends down hesitantly and grabs one end of the roll, and we drag it out of the flat, down the staircase, out through the front door and then lay it next to the wheelie bin. When Max hears the thing being dragged through the hallway he comes out to help us, though there isn't much he can do except open the front door for us. We go back upstairs and Max looks around the 'living room', trying to envision it as his studio. It's a big room, without any furniture, so there'd be plenty of space for him. But there's a big hole in the ceiling/roof where the rain pisses in, a broken window where the wind blows in, a big hole in one wall where a fireplace was removed, and the room is very damp and mouldy and littered with mouse droppings. Not ideal then - and yet he's not completely put off. He has reservations more about the bedroom, which is understandable, and he's going to have to think about it and let me know. We have a brew, then they set off back into town on their bikes, and it's time for me to head back to the Swinny to do an evening shift so I get in the car and drive down the road, pipping the horn and waving to Max and Jaz as I overtake them at Stair.

An evening shift isn't much different to a lunchtime shift, except that the menu is a bit different. Again it's fairly quiet, this being a Tuesday and still in the quiet season, and there isn't much of a workload – although it is still a bit stressful due to Billy's difficult ways. He would make life simpler for everyone if he could just be a bit friendlier, but no, he has to assume the role of the arrogant and insulting chef, some kind of control freak who gets his kicks by putting other people down, and it really is all very tedious and it's not as much fun as it used to be working at the tea shop – in fact it's no fun at all and I can't see myself sticking at the job, to be honest.

the face of the devil

Another day, another dollar, or pound or whatever – except that there aren't many pounds being earned to justify sacrificing my precious time in skivvying at the Swinny for miserable Billy... And now it's Wednesday and I've just earned another three hours of pay for a lunchtime stint and I'm back at the house, warming my hands against the oil-filled radiator and waiting for the kettle to boil and waiting for Bea and Jess to come and visit me.

And lo and behold at 3pm I hear the front door bang shut and then a rapping on the flat door. I told them the other evening to just come up and look out for the door with the brass knocker that looks like it's the face of the devil. 'Hello and welcome to the scary madhouse that is falling down. And Jess, how would you like to share this flat with me – if Max decides he doesn't want to?' (And Max has had time to sleep on it and he isn't exactly jumping at the opportunity.) The pair of them have a good look round and then the three of us sit round the table in the Yellow Room and we have some celery soup that I've just made, along with some spicy vegetable pate and wholemeal bread. They've walked all the way from Keswick and are grateful for some sustenance. They gabble on like a pair of excited teenagers, which is what they're usually like when they're together – best friends, kindred spirits, and possibly even lovers. Although I'm their host I feel a bit left out of their special relationship and I wish it was just Bea on her own here with me. I don't think I'd want to share the flat with Jess, even if she wanted to share with me, because I find her a bit irritating the way she gabbles on without listening, her mind flitting all over the place – but she probably wouldn't want to move in here anyway because it's a dump and it's too far out of town for someone who doesn't even have a bike, never mind a car. She's glad she came to have a look though because the place is...well it's *interesting*, isn't it? – *fascinating* in fact. But who in their right mind would want to actually *live* here?

I give the girls a lift back into town in the old green V-dub. I ripped the back seat out a while ago because it was very damp and so, whilst Bea sits beside me in the passenger seat, Jess sits on a piece of hardboard in the back, without a seatbelt but also without a care, as we wind our way down the valley to Keswick. I don't know what's going on with the clutch or gears or whatever it is but it's almost impossible to engage first and second gears in this car. That means I have to give it plenty of revs when I set off in third gear or when I'm going up a hill in third gear – third and fourth being the only usable gears. Sometimes I manage to yank the gear stick into second, but it demands so much force that I fear I will break the stick, so I've pretty much given up on that. Anyways, we make it into town and I drop them off and remind Bea that we are meeting for a 'writers' meet' tomorrow afternoon in the George. 'Looking forward to it,' she says. And then I drive round to the supermarket to stock up on a few bits and bobs. And then it's back to the purple castle, a quick brew and then back to work at the Swinny.

the dharma bums

The evening shift at the Swinny is very quiet and so they let me go at 8pm. When I get back to the house I can hear loud music coming from Ray's room. When I get to the landing at the top of the stairs I peer through the hole in the door and shout 'hello'. I can see him pacing up and down with a glass of drink in his hand. He lets me in and he seems to be in a friendly mood. There's a quarter-full bottle of sherry on the desk and the speakers are blasting out the soundtrack to the musical *Cabaret*. He turns down the volume and asks me if I've had a good day. And then he tells me that he's had a very bad one. He had to go and visit the doctor in town, and the doctor told him that he is to be 'sectioned' and that 'the men in the white coats' would be coming to take him away in the morning. His mother had arranged it all.

I remember the first time I met Ray, which was when I first lived in this house back in '93, and when I knew him as 'Adam' (and I'm going to call him Adam from now on, which is his real name, even if he does prefer 'Ray', or sometimes 'Peter'). I was in the kitchen doing something when he came in and introduced himself. He must have been in his late-forties then, at a guess, and he looked pretty much as he does now – grey hair, grey straggly beard, and a bit red in the face. He was relatively sane then, although officially 'mentally ill'. He was just staying in the house for a few days before resuming his wandering existence - like an old-fashioned tramp. He was an intelligent guy, but he didn't want to live a normal life in society, with a job and a house and a wife and all the usual material trappings. He was like some kind of dharma bum, although I don't know what his dharma was or is (although I do know that he is spiritually-minded and he likes Krishnamurti). I remember him ranting on about how his desire to be constantly travelling around was equated by the authorities with mental illness, and that after living in 'cardboard city' for a while he ended up being taken away to live in a psychiatric hospital, and then a 'halfway house' for a while. 'It's not *me* that's mad,' he said. 'It's *them*!' 'I just want to be free to be a tramp, but they won't let me...I don't *want* a house, I don't *want* a car, I don't *want* a television...I just want to be free to travel around and live simply.'

And when I think of my own life – all the wandering around, the different jobs and addresses, I wonder if I'm not that much different to Adam. It's just a difference of degree I suppose. Although I'm a wanderer I do like to have a roof over my head and some material possessions and so I go out to work in jobs which I don't really want to do but which provide me with these things. My own wanderings might be regarded with suspicion by some, but I am nevertheless a part of society, though to some degree also a dharma bum. And what is *my* dharma? Well, it has to do with my *writing*...

the men in the white coats

In the morning I'm sitting at my desk in the Yellow Room, reading the problematical early chapter of 'Black Sail'. With a pencil I draw lines through sections of text and write 'too nakedly autobiographical.' And yet, I'm not sure... My writing is *supposed to be autobiographical*, and honest – so what's the problem? Some of the material makes me cringe and I score these definite diagonal lines through passages and note 'not untrue, but I don't think it belongs here.' So *that's* the problem – that some passages are *not relevant* to the story at hand. There's too much painful-to-read life-history back story that is bogging down the forward momentum of the narrative. It's not necessary or appropriate to tell 'all that David Copperfield kind of crap', as Holden Caulfield once put it, but just the stuff that is relevant to Black Sail. Some of the material is relevant, and I put pencil ticks and 'OK' in the margin, but I think I'm going to have to ditch large chunks of this chapter, and use the good and relevant bits for a later chapter.

My thoughts are disturbed by a loud banging on the front door. I look at my wristwatch and it's 10am. Again the loud banging on the door. I get up from my chair and go out the flat and down the stairs to see who it is. And when I open the door I am confronted by two uniformed police officers, and also a smartly-dressed man in a tweed jacket, collar and tie. 'We've come for Adam Vergauwen,' says the man in the tweed jacket. I invite them over the threshold and leave them standing in the hallway, whilst I go back up the stairs to tell Adam. I can see straight into his room through the hole in the door so there's no need to knock, and I can see that he's not in there. I call out his name anyway, 'Adam!' And then I check the bathroom and kitchen, but he's not in there either, so I go back downstairs. 'He might be down below,' I say, and I open the door in the hallway that leads down to Mrs Vee's basement flat. I rap on her door and call out 'Mrs Vee!' and 'Adam!', but there's no answer. I saw the old lady get into a taxi outside the front of the house about an hour ago, when I was in my kitchen getting a coffee. She was probably going food shopping in town, and I guess she's not back yet. But I haven't seen or heard Adam. I tell this to the three men and they ask to see Adam's room so I take them up and I go back into the flat. I can hear them talking next door, and also the sound of a police radio. I can't concentrate on my writing now, but I've got to go to work at the Swinny soon anyway. They knock on my door and ask me to get in touch with the police station if I see him, and then they drive off in their police car. And shortly afterwards I get in my own car and drive the short distance to work. Usually I'd cycle for the day shift, but today I'm going straight into town afterwards to meet Bea at The George.

where is home?

Sitting in The George now with a pint of Jennings Bitter it's 2.55pm, and I'm waiting for Bea to arrive. I'm in the room to the left of the front door, sitting at a table in a sort of wooden booth. I've told Bea that I know a couple of other writers in town, and that this could evolve into a proper group, but to be honest I am more interested in just a one-to-one with her. I've written down some notes in my journal book as to what we could talk about with regard to writing, and also I'm going to suggest that we do a ten minute timed writing exercise on a particular theme.

She arrives a little after 3pm and gets her own drink – also a pint of ale, and sits down opposite me in the wooden booth. She asks me about the Purple House and the job at the Swinny, and tells me about her job at the youth hostel and the people she works with.

She's been going out with one of the lads who works at the Keswick hostel, but she says she's finished with him. He's quite a bit younger than me, and younger than her too – *too* young perhaps for what she wants. She smiles at me and I think she looks very attractive – round face, pale complexion, brown hair down to her shoulders, big brown intelligent eyes, and a mischievous sexy smile. It's warm in the pub, from the open fire, and she takes off her light blue fleece hoody to reveal a maroon tee-shirt – which shows off the curves of her largish breasts to better effect. She's a buxom lass, which is good in my books. And we need to talk about books, or at least *writing*, if we are to do what we are supposed to be doing here today. I ask her about her reading interests, and her writing experience and aspirations. She says she likes Douglas Coupland, and recommends *Girlfriend in a Coma*. She's been to uni and got herself a degree in English, albeit a 'Third' – which she feels a bit embarrassed about, but I tell her it doesn't matter. I started an English degree course myself but I dropped out, though being on the course for a while was useful – if only to show how useless the higher education system is, especially in a course like English Literature. Okay, you may come across a few books that are worth reading, and your critical skills will be sharpened, but your literary creativity will probably be discouraged and frustrated. The only creative writing that will be considered valid is that which demonstrates that the student has absorbed the prescribed theories of literature from the lectures and seminars and academic texts, thus showing that the teaching staff and the higher education industry is succeeding at turning out brainwashed clones – which is their aim. So, to only score a third class degree is nothing to be ashamed of; in fact I think it might even be an indicator of depth and individuality. Bea has dabbled at writing short stories and poems but, like so many English graduates, she lacks confidence in her ability, and is even a little distrustful of her impulse to do it. So much for so-called 'education' - which is supposed to be about *drawing out* a person's ability, not stifling it.

Anyways, it's time to do a little exercise...time to engage with 'wild mind', rather than the conditioned, self-critical, civilised mind... I suggest to Bea that we both write for ten minutes on the subject 'home'. The idea is to keep the hand moving, to keep the pen moving across the page as far as possible, which is to say writing fairly *quickly*, and thereby admitting 'unconscious' mind, *wild* mind, and expressing whatever comes up on the subject 'home'. I set the stopwatch on my trusty Casio and say 'Go!' and away we go, scribbling in our notebooks, writing about what 'home' means to us.

What is 'home' to me? *Where* is home? I don't really have one in the literal sense. I left my parental home, the home where I grew up, at the age of eighteen, and then it ceased to be my home. My old bedroom was swiftly converted into my father's 'office'. Since then I have had an extraordinary number of addresses, usually just rented rooms, or sometimes flats, but none of them lived in long enough to really constitute a home. I was always pretty much just passing through – and still am. When I lived with a girlfriend in a place for over a year - that almost felt like a home, but again it was only rented, only temporary, and it never really felt like 'ours'. I suppose I consider the Lake District in general to be my home. The fells and the towns and villages are all my home, and the actual addresses, the brick/stone/wood shelters, the buildings with their postcodes are not of any real consequence...except that there have been some special ones – such as Black Sail and Rigg Beck, for instance. And yet I am not so attached to the Lakes that I wouldn't consider moving down to the West Country, or anywhere else, should my heart or instinct lead me that way for whatever reason – which might simply be to see the world afresh. And being able to see the world afresh is important for a writer. Moving around enables this. In our settled day-to-day routines of work and play and staying in one place, in one job, we can become stuck – stuck in a rut of limited perception and limited expression. Being able to take a step back and to see the world afresh, like a poet, or indeed *as* a poet – this in itself is a sort of home, the home of *writing*. The whole world is a home really. I am a citizen of the English Lake District, but I belong ultimately to the Earth, and I feel no particular allegiance to my country, the 'United Kingdom' (which is a fiction). The Lakes is my adopted 'home', but *writing* is perhaps a greater home, and if my muse bids me to re-locate to Cornwall in the service of my writing, then to Cornwall I will go.

Time's up, we put our pens down, and we read what we've written to each other. Bea has written about a more literal conception of home – the house where she grew up with her parents and sister in South Manchester. From what she's written I get a good idea of how close she is to her family – especially her father and sister. She describes the house and the nearby countryside, walking along the canal with the family dog, going out on the town with her sister, sitting in the garden with her father... Her family home is still very important to her and she often goes back home to visit her folks. Her bedroom, the room where she grew up is still there for her. Her parents and sister are still there for her. The seasonal job at the youth hostel and the room at the house on Ratcliffe Place are just temporary. Like most YHA assistant wardens she's just doing this as a sort of 'stop-gap' whilst she makes up her mind what she really wants to do – which will probably be some kind of 'professional' career job that will necessitate going back to university for vocational training, and which will also necessitate going back to live in Manchester, or some other city. Then again, she might just opt to be a Lakeland 'drop-out' like me...

'What do you want to do with your life?' I ask her. 'I dunno... Probably something in the caring professions – like occupational therapy, or physiotherapy... Something useful to society, and something that pays a lot better than YHA.' Ah yes, the *money*...and of course she's a middle-class girl who expects a certain 'standard of living', and if she ever gets hitched with somebody she'll expect him to have a similar standard of living, and also to keep her at that standard should she cease to work because she becomes a mother... She's only twenty-five years old now, and she still acts like a student, but time marches on and she's going to want to get herself sorted out and settled at some point. And I wonder how attractive I am to her as a 'drop-out'. I'm a writer, but I've not made it yet... She likes my company, and I can feel this chemistry between us, but I'm not much of a catch for a nice middle-class girl who says her favourite pastime is 'eating out'. She may be a bit alternative and she says she's a feminist (and also used to be a lesbian), but I think she still wants to be wined and dined in the old-fashioned conventional way, and as she gets older she will want to settle down with someone 'professional' (monied). But for the time being she is still young and relatively adventurous and carefree. 'Would you like another pint?' I ask her. 'I shouldn't really, I'm back at work at five 'o clock – but go on then.' Working for the YHA offers 'respectability without responsibility', as Max once put it. It sounds good when you tell people what you do, and it looks good on a CV – better than 'kitchen assistant' for example (and yet there aint really much difference).

As I walk to the bar for our drinks Jess walks in, and so I offer to buy one for her too. And then when I take the drinks back to our table Bea and Jess are chattering away excitedly about some YHA politics or something. Bea had told Jess that we were going to be here for a writers' meet, and apparently Jess is keen to join us for our next meeting. I quite like Jess, but I'm a bit non-plussed by her joining us just now – just as I was feeling something building between me and Bea. Jess tells me that she's *not* interested in renting the room in the flat at Rigg Beck, and that she's found a room to rent at a house in town. We drink our drinks and then the time comes to make tracks and the two girls go back to Ratcliffe Place, and I head back to Rigg Beck.

what is rent?

As I walk up the stairs I see that the flat door is open, which is strange. I walk through and find Mrs Vee standing in the middle of the kitchen, wearing a silly purple hat and stinking of stale pee. I had definitely locked the door, so she must have a spare key (which she said she didn't). Obviously I'm not too pleased to find her snooping around, but I'm not in the mood for a confrontation. She tells me that one of her London friends is coming up in a couple of weeks' time to do roofing and other work on the house, starting with the flat, and therefore she doesn't want to let the flat to me anymore. 'Have you got any rent for me? It's time you started paying rent.' I've been in the flat for four weeks now and I haven't paid any rent. I've been working at the Swinny, but I haven't done a lot of hours and I don't have any rent money. I've spent my money on food and drink and petrol and taxing the car and a new pair of fell shoes, and I don't have any left. 'Sorry, I don't have any.' Even if I did have the money I'd be reluctant to pay her. She's messed me about, changing her mind about how much the rent for the flat should be, and now she's going to kick me out. I'm outwardly calm about it, but inwardly my anger is building. What is *rent*? Money demanded by people with property, capital, money, the 'haves' from the 'have-*nots*' in order to accumulate more money. And I'm reluctant to pay her any rent for this decrepit flat. 'Haven't you got *any*?' she says in her high-pitched patronising voice. 'I haven't done many hours at the pub, and I get paid a week in hand and I had to tax the car...' She looks at me with a disbelieving half-smile, and I know that in a way I am 'guilty'. I am the non-rent-paying fugitive from various creditors and a 'writer' prepared to rip other people off in order to try and achieve his own 'selfish' artistic ends, and yet, ironically, not having done much work at all on my creative mission for weeks now – since living here at Rigg Beck. Living here has been such an issue in itself.

might go feral

So that's it now – my days here at Rigg Beck are numbered, and pretty soon I'm going to be homeless, unless I can find somewhere else – but without money for a deposit I'm not optimistic. Without accommodation round here I won't be able to keep my job at the Swinny – but that won't be any great loss. If I can find somewhere to store all my gear I might just go feral for a while and camp out in the fells. I wouldn't have to pay rent to anybody, although I'd be struggling for food and I'd have no 'room to write'.

Today is a day off and I'm driving down to South Lakes to see about a part-time cleaning job on a National Trust campsite. Apparently there's accommodation provided – in the form of an old caravan on the site. It's quite a pleasant mild late-April day with some sunshine and new-born lambs jumping around in the fields, and it's an enjoyable drive down the old A591, over the Raise, past Grasmere, through Ambleside, and then it's the Hawkshead road, and then the turn off for Low Wray. This is near where I used to lodge with my old running club friend (and where I wrote 'Only Human'), but I've never visited the campsite before.

I report to the office, where I meet an officious little Welshman who is dressed in National Trust green uniform and wellington boots, and who introduces himself as 'Dillwyn'. He takes me to the caravan, which is a big old brown thing that has seen better days. There are some trees to the back of it, but it's on the edge of a car park, and close to a toilet block, so not ideal for someone who likes quietness and privacy, but beggars can't be choosers and I am a beggar and it's *something* – which I suppose is better than nothing. Dillwyn unlocks the door to the caravan and we step inside. It's warm inside and it smells very musty. There's loads of space, but there's no running water, no cooking facility, and every surface is covered with specks of black mould. Dillwyn says that last season there were no less than five campsite wardens living in here, but now they are accommodated in a cottage by the office. Five people! That would've been ridiculously cramped. If I get the job I'll have the place to myself, my own little mouldy metal flat. Dillwyn is full of health-and-safety speak and seems to be concerned mainly about the lack of a fire extinguisher in the caravan. He says he'll make sure he gets one. And I'm thinking well *great!* No running water, no cooker, mould everywhere, but at least I'll have a fire extinguisher! I guess the mould will clean off, and I'll be able to get water from the toilet block, and I could use my camping stove, but really the place is a hovel and no-one should be expected to live in such a place. But this is how the National Trust treat their staff – you are expected to put up with such things because you are expected to be committed to the Trust as some kind of cause. You are expected to work for a pittance, if indeed you get paid at all (many of them being volunteers), in the hope that you will be able to work up through the ranks and get yourself the status of a proper paid job as a 'ranger' or whatever, proudly wearing your green uniform and obeying all the instructions from your superiors at the head office, all the highly-paid directors and managers with their clipped southern accents and their double-barrelled surnames and their constantly changing missions and marketing strategies. My god, it's even worse than the YHA – and that's saying something! And maybe I'll be better off camping in the fells after all, or maybe living in a cave like Millican Dalton, or even building my own little wooden shack in the middle of Ennerdale Forest and hoping that the Forestry Commission won't notice. It would be great if you could just set up home anywhere – like in the old pioneering days in North America or Australia, or even Dartmoor – where you were once allowed to set up home anywhere on the moor, as long as you could build your house in one day. But unfortunately this is the twenty-first century and this is 'Great Britain' and this is the Lake District and everything is owned and strictly controlled and you haven't got a hope in hell of finding somewhere decent to live unless you've got pots of money.

things just happen

Back at the house I feel like getting drunk, so I knock back a fair bit of red wine with my simple pasta dinner and then head into town in the old V-dub. I don't know how long she's going to last with this clutch problem, but I hope she lasts long enough to transport me and my gear to the next place when the time comes to leave Rigg Beck. I hope she lasts long enough to get me into town tonight because I want to see people and I want to see life... In fact I particularly want to see Bea.

At Stair I drive past the entrance to the Adventure Centre and then turn right at the lane for Little Town. I drive up here just a little way and then park up just past the village hall, by the phone box. I fumble for some coins in the zippered pouch of my fabric wallet and then dial the number for Ratcliffe Place. It's

8.45pm and she should be back home now after the evening shift, and *yes*, she answers the phone, and *yes*, she *would* like to go for a drink with me at The George. 'I'm on my way,' I say, and I get back into the car, turn the key, reverse down into the little car park to turn around, then give her plenty of revs and lurch forwards in third gear towards Keswick.

I call round at Ratcliffe Place and she answers the door with a big smile on her face, says 'just a minute' as she grabs her hoody and pulls it on (giving me a glimpse of her bare midriff as her tee-shirt rides up a bit), and then we're strolling into town together in the cool evening air. It's only a few minutes' walk to The George, and it's not too busy in there and we seat ourselves at a table in a cosy corner, me with a pint of Jennings ale, and Bea with a large glass of red wine. She looks radiant with a happy youthful energy and I want to kiss her. But no, not yet... She says she enjoyed our 'writers' meet' and looks forward to doing it again. She also says she enjoyed reading the first chapter of 'Black Sail' (which I gave to her just yesterday), and she's keen to read some more – which is good. She might be able to help me knock it into better shape if she does a close critical reading. I've not shown it to anyone else yet and I could do with a reader – someone who appreciates, who 'gets' the writing, but who would not be afraid to speak her mind if she finds what she thinks are weak points, or mistakes in spelling or whatever. She might be a great help. And she says she's written a short piece herself just this very day – about her fairly recent meditation retreat at a Buddhist monastery – and she'll show it to me next time we have our writers' meet. She's into

Buddhism and meditation. She's done a few courses and read a few books and she tries to meditate each day. She tells me that she suffers from depression and anxiety and she's trying to control it, or 'manage' it, with meditation. She never struck me as a depressive, though I realised she was a deep thinker, a thoughtful and spiritually-minded person. A *kindred*, in some ways perhaps... I used to meditate a bit myself, and I've 'dabbled' with Buddhism, but I suppose I regard my running as a meditation nowadays, and I'm not into subscribing to any 'isms'. But cultivating the ability to watch your own thoughts, so that you are fully aware of all the stuff that arises in your mind seems to me to be a very worthwhile path to follow. Know thyself, be thyself and *express* thyself...and for me 'the path' is *writing*, rather than meditation (although it could be said that writing is itself a sort of meditation, especially if it is writing of the wild mind variety – that is writing 'without consciousness').

Bea takes a sip of red wine from the large glass. Actually it's more than a sip – more of a gulp. She likes a drink and she's enjoying herself and she's not going to be careful or frugal. Why should she? She may be into Buddhism, but she is also young and relatively carefree and why should she hold back? She looks beautiful as she raises the glass to her lips, her brown hair hanging down, her throat muscles moving under the pale skin of her neck as she swallows the wine. And then she carefully puts the glass down on the polished wooden table and turns to smile at me, and she looks happy – happy to be here, here and now with me, as I am with her. Present moment, wonderful moment. Those deep brown eyes hold a mystery, the mystery of her soul that is unknowable, but which I intend to get to know – as far as it is possible. Her mouth is quite small, but perfectly formed, the insides of the pink curves of her lips slightly coated and glistening with the wine. As she smiles I get the flash of her white teeth, all even, straight, unblemished. 'Are you okay?' she asks me. 'Oh yes,' I say, and I realise that I've just been in a trance.

I gulp down a goodly amount of ale, and why should *I* hold back? The smooth, dark and nutty ale slips down a treat and I'm feeling mellow, although also a little anxious in anticipation of getting closer to this girl, this woman. There's something happening – an awakening in my heart and my loins, which is exciting. 'I admire your dedication to your writing,' she says. 'It's the only way,' I say. 'You have to really stick at it if you want to get anywhere. Ideally you need to write every day, or nearly every day – even if it's just a journal entry or a short sketch, or maybe a poem.' 'And I like your *style* of writing,' she says. 'It's so direct and honest and speech-like. And the way you mix the down-to-earth with the spiritual...' 'Good,' I say, 'I'm glad you like it, glad that you *get* it.'

We drain our glasses and I go to the bar for more. As I bring the drinks back to our table and see Bea sitting there smiling and looking very comfortable, it feels like she could be my girlfriend. 'When did you last have a girlfriend?' she asks me, and it seems like a 'loaded question' and also a question that makes me feel on trial. I have to think about it for a moment. 'Two-and-a-half years ago – when I was with Lucia in

Devon, before I moved back up here to work at Black Sail.' Two-and-a-half years! It's a long time, is it not? And perhaps Bea will think there's something wrong with me for it to have been so long. After all, the last time she had a boyfriend was only last week. But then again, it could be considered a plus point that I've been on my own for a long time, because I don't go out with just *anybody*. I've had a couple of very short-lived flings since then, but I've not had a proper 'going out with' relationship – just because I've not happened to meet anyone suitable. I guess that's what it comes down to: suitability. It's also true that I've not made much effort to find someone, but I guess that's because I think it's better if something 'just happens', without going searching for it, as things have 'just happened' for me in the past. It's probably also true that things are less likely to 'just happen' as I've got older, and also as I've moved around a lot, living the life of the impecunious vagabond-writer – which, let's face it, is not usually attractive to women. But Bea is attracted to me, I can tell.

Finally we leave the pub and walk back to Ratcliffe Place. I've had too much to drink to drive back to Rigg Beck, and so I call for a taxi from the phone in the house. The young dope-smokers (one of whom is Bea's ex-boyfriend) are in the living room watching TV and smoking dope and so Bea and I decide to stand outside in the street to wait for the taxi. It's pretty quiet here, not being on any main thoroughfare and just the occasional car or pedestrian goes past. We stand side by side on the pavement and wait. 'What a beautiful night!' says Bea, as she looks skywards to admire the stars. 'That's Orion, and that's The Plough, and that bright star there is Sirius.' There isn't much light pollution from this small town and you can see the constellations clearly in the deep blue-sky. She shivers in the cool air. 'Are you cold?' I ask, and reach for her hand. We hold hands and I move closer to her side. I can hear her deep rhythmic breathing and see her breath come out in little clouds of steam. And I can see her chest gently rising and falling as she's breathing – in, out, deep, slow... I pull her towards me so that we are facing each other, inches away from each other, and I look into her expectant eyes and at her half-open lips, and I kiss her. She makes no resistance and I put my arms around her and she puts her arms around me and we meld together in a beautiful long and delicious snog.

The taxi pulls up a few yards away and we pull away from the kiss, but continue to hold each other. She smiles and I smile. Her breathing is deep and steady. 'Are you doing anything tomorrow afternoon?' I ask her. 'No. Come round, if you like.' 'Okay then. See you tomorrow!' And I give her a quick goodnight peck and get into the taxi and head back to Rigg Beck.

no man is an island

In the morning I'm feeling hungover as I sit at my desk, unable to concentrate on my writing, when there's a rap at the door and I don't have the presence of mind to ignore it so I get up and open the door to Mrs Vee – who stands in the hallway stinking, a couple of flies buzzing around her head, as she tells me that she wants me out of here in a week's time at the latest, and also that she's locked the front door of the house 'for security of Adam's room', so that I'll have to go in and out of the house by the *back* door, which means going down the basement staircase and right past her own living accommodation, which'll make it harder to come and go discreetly.

After I've got rid of her I get a couple of bits and bobs together in a small rucksack and set off walking down the road, into Keswick. At Stair I go to the phone box and phone in 'sick' to the Swinny, and then – rather than carry on walking along the road that would take me past the Swinny – I carry on walking up the lane to Little Town, then up through the disused mine workings to Hause Gate (with Cat Bells on my left and a great view of Derwent Water in front of me), then down the bridleway and through some woods to a path along the shore of the lake. It's a beautiful walk along this western shore of Derwent Water, the path passing mainly through woodland – with some magnificent old Scots Pines and winding round lots of little bays. At one point, Brandelhow Point, there's a big house almost hidden in the trees, and seemingly on its own little island, although connected to the 'mainland' by a narrow strip of land. 'No man is an Island, entire of itself; every man is a piece of the Continent, a part of the main...' There are four islands at the Keswick end of the lake – Derwent Isle, Lord's, Rampsholme and St. Herbert's Island (where anchorite priest, 'The Hermit of Derwentwater' dwelt for many years in the middle of the 7th century 'to avoid the intercourse of man, and that nothing might withdraw his attention from unceasing mortification and prayer'). There are also a few tiny islands such as Otter Island in Abbot's Bay on the other side of this point, and also a floating island at the southern end of the lake, which is forced from the lake bed to the surface at infrequent intervals by gases generated by the decomposition of the tangled vegetation of which it is formed. The floating island normally appears towards the end of a warm summer, and can stay buoyant for several weeks or even months before it sinks back down to the lake bed (which is only about six feet deep at this point). Back in August of '93, just before I left Rigg Beck to move to the Duddon Valley, I was vaguely thinking about 'going feral' and looking for places where I could live for free and I had this crazy idea of camping on the floating island – which had just made it's appearance. It seemed like the ultimate transient place to live – a little patch of land that came and went, an island surrounded on all sides and underneath by water, and not owned by anybody (although the National Trust would probably claim it as their own). It would have been singularly precarious, prone to sinking without warning at the end of the season – although perhaps no more precarious than living in the Purple House, which might suddenly fall down at any moment. Anyways, back to the house at Brandlehow Point... During that first stay at the Purple House in '93 I once visited this house by appointment – to view a private library of New Age books. I think the owner was some kind of holistic therapist and she had this big collection of books that she wanted to share with others and you could phone her up and arrange to go there for a browse and borrow books, like in a public library. I don't know if she's still there, or if the library is still there.

Further along the path, in amongst the woods, is a cottage that always seems to be empty. It's probably a holiday cottage or 'second home'. I remember Sharon seriously thinking about squatting in the place when she had to leave her digs on the other side of the lake. I think that in those days you could still legally squat in a property if it had been uninhabited for a long time – although of course you can't do that nowadays. There are loads of these second homes all over the Lakes that are hardly ever used. This one here in the woods has got a 'Neighbourhood Watch' sticker in the window, although where the nearest neighbours are I don't know. But if a homeless person were to break in and try and live here the police would soon find out about it – they'd be round in a matter of days and the homeless person would be charged with one thing or another and they'd have to go to court and be criminalised and there'd be a report in the Keswick Reminder and the good people of Keswick would shake their heads at the audacity of this individual who thought he/she could live in someone else's property without paying rent or council tax, and the owner of the property (who perhaps only usually uses it for a couple of weeks in the year) will decide to invest in greater security measures and ask someone they trust who lives locally to keep a regular eye on the place in an attempt to prevent any further occurrences of the crime.

A little further on I hear the sound of a saxophone and I come across a man playing said instrument as he stands on a rocky promontory, looking out over the lake – playing some kind of mellow soulful jazz tune to himself and to any passing walker such as myself, or to the group of kayakers who are paddling out in the lake (which reminds me that one time Purple House resident and Black Sail warden – Mack – used to kayak across the lake to go to work at the Derwentwater youth hostel when he lived at the house, which is a pretty cool way to commute). The lake is about a mile wide at this point. The average depth of the lake is only eighteen feet, which makes it by far the shallowest of the lakes in the Lake District, and one of the first to freeze over in winter.

The lakeshore path terminates at the Hawes End outdoor centre, but it's only a short distance on tarmac before I pick up another very pleasant path through woodland, and through the grounds of Lingholm Gardens. I stop for a while to have a drink from my water bottle and just appreciate my surroundings, and also try and meditate for five or ten minutes. But meditation is out of the question because I'm feeling quite wired from last night's drinking and then that passionate kiss, and also wired from the cafetiere of strong coffee that I drank before setting off on this walk. The gentle pace of the walk through beautiful surroundings is having a positive and revitalising effect on me, but my mind is hardly what you could call calm or centred. I'm excited about seeing Bea again.

Onwards I march through Portinscale, over the suspension bridge and through the fields into town. I've got a little time to kill before I meet Bea, so I call at the Tourist Information Centre (in the Moot Hall) to say hello to Max, but he's busy with a queue of customers getting him to sort out their holiday accommodation or with queries about tourist attractions of one sort or another. So I go for a coffee in the cafe called 'Pillars', which overlooks Market Place. I take a seat by the window and enjoy watching the world go by as I sip my black coffee. More coffee! It's a Saturday today, which means it's market day and Keswick is thronging with folk. 'Gay thrang', if you like. The Keswick Jazz Festival is on at the moment – which will account for a lot of visitors, and also for the lakeshore saxophonist. The open air market is pretty lively with stalls selling cheese and bread and cakes and all manner of locally-produced food, and stalls with books, clothes, shoes, jewellery (where Lila once stole a bracelet) and all sorts of other things, and I reckon it's nice to see a vibrant old-fashioned open-air market like this one – which makes a change from just outdoor shops or the usual corporate chain stores. Anyway, it's time to go to Ratcliffe Place so I gulp down the last of the coffee and say a cheery 'bye' to the ladies behind the counter, then it's down the stairs and into the throng, and wending my way up St. John Street, past The George on my left and The Printer's Pie stationary shop on my right, then left down Church Street until it opens up into a sort of square, where a number of streets converge. There's the old green V-dub parked outside the staff house and looking pretty tatty, but also quite cool I think. 'Cool'. I realise that I've just voiced this word in my head again, and it's not a word I use very often but I wonder if I've started using it because Bea uses it a lot, being younger than me. Next thing you know I'll be wearing a hoody.

the stuff of life

I knock on the door and I don't have to wait long before she opens it, and there she is in her bare feet, wearing dark blue jeans and a black vest top which shows off her smooth pale womanly arms and also the curves of her breasts pushing out against the tight fabric. She smiles, and I smile back and - a little unsure of myself – I kiss her awkwardly on the cheek and we have a little hug. 'I enjoyed last night,' she says. 'Yes, me too. We'll have to do it again some time.' 'That would be nice.' She leads me through the living room into the kitchen. 'Are you hungry?' she asks. 'I am.' 'Good, because I've made some salad stuff. I finished work earlier than usual, so I thought I'd make us some nice lunch.' 'Cool. I'm ready to eat when you are.' And so she produces these bowls of things she's prepared and starts arranging stuff on plates: lettuce leaves, sliced tomato, cucumber and avocado, and a feta cheese, olive and red onion salad. It looks fantastic – just my kind of food. And there's some Bryson's sunflower wholemeal bread to go with it. She's got good taste. Am I obsessed with food, dear reader? I make no apologies. Food is the stuff of life – food and sex...

And so we sit down at the table in the living room to eat, and I really appreciate the effort that she's put in to create this healthy tasty food. Salad stuff can make you feel good straight away and I certainly feel good eating this. My hangover has gone. It must be the 'raw energy', and also perhaps the energy between me and Bea. She says that she was a bit hungover too, but that she's okay now – and she certainly looks okay. She looks ravishing, in fact. After our meal she makes us both a peppermint tea and she takes me upstairs to show me her room.

It's a medium-sized room with the usual single bed, wardrobe, chest of drawers, desk, hard chair and also an antique Lloyd Loom wicker chair. There are a number of postcards and photos (including some of New Zealand, where she went travelling over the winter) blue-tacked to the wardrobe doors. Being on the top floor the ceiling is sloped at one side, and the window overlooks the grey stone buildings of Keswick. There's a substantial-looking hi-fi system sitting on the chest of drawers, a stack of CDs, a few books, and a small wooden Buddha. Her work clothes are draped over the back of the hard chair and there are some papers on the desk – including the typescript of the first chapter of 'Black Sail'. I sit in the wicker chair and she puts on some music – a Massive Attack CD. She sits on the edge of the single bed and we listen to the music and talk about what kind of music we like to listen to and what sort of books we like to read and what sort of films we like to watch. The movies are a bit of a blank for me, so that's a bit of a conversation-stopper, but we decide that we will go to one of the art house films that they sometimes put on at the local Alhambra cinema. She asks me about the Purple House and I tell her that I've got to move out in a week's time. She's concerned for me. 'But what are you going to do?' 'I don't know. Maybe go and live in a mouldy caravan near Ambleside and work for the National Trust. Or maybe live in a cave on Castle Crag. I don't know yet. But I don't want to think about it or talk about it just now...' 'Okay, fair enough.' We sip our peppermint tea and listen to the music. Currently playing is the track *Teardrop* – which is one of my favourites. I get up from the chair and look through Bea's CD collection. Being a Mancunian she likes quite a few Manchester bands, like The Smiths and New Order and The Stone Roses. And then I see the recently-released album *Lost Souls* by Doves. 'Shall we listen to this?' 'Yeah, put that on,' she agrees enthusiastically. I remove the CD from the case, slide it into the drawer on the hi-fi and press the 'play' button. The opening track, an instrumental called *firesuite* comes on. Echoey guitars warming up, fading in, the sound of a fire burning in the background... 'Bring me the remote control,' she says, and so I pick it up and take it to her, and decide I might as well take the liberty of sitting next to her on the edge of the bed. 'Do you mind if I sit here?' I ask her, and she laughs and says 'No, of course not' and so I sit next to her and she touches my leg affectionately. I turn to her and cautiously run my fingers through her hair. She smiles and moves in closer to me. I put my arm around her and move my face close to hers. She turns to face me and we kiss, a little awkwardly at first, and then more naturally. We pull away and change our sitting positions slightly to make it easier, and then we kiss again, and it turns into a long and passionate snog. I can hear her breathing getting heavier and feel the rise and fall of her chest and smell the natural smell of her hair combined with the sweet coconutty fragrance of some soap or body lotion or something. And this track *firesuite* is washing over me, through me, guitars and drums building up a rhythm and a tension, a sense of expectancy, an echoing voice, a touch of piano - beautiful abstract spiritual music taking me on an inner flight that is just right for the occasion. We pull away again and she moves back further onto the bed and lies down and playfully tugs at my tee-shirt to join her. And so I take off my shoes and do just that, and we kiss again, our hands moving and exploring each others' bodies. The pale skin of her midriff is soft and smooth and warm to the touch, but I want to see and feel more of her so I peel the black vest upwards and she raises her arms to help me take it off over her head. And then I unhook the bra and remove that too and her bare breasts look fantastic. I hold them and kiss them and suck at her nipples. She's breathing heavily and she makes a little 'mmm' of appreciation. I take off my own top and she fumbles at the button and fly of my jeans and grabs at the waistband. Finally we strip ourselves off entirely and roll around naked on the bed, passionately kissing and fondling each other, the uplifting soundtrack by *Doves* in the background. She looks great naked and she must be very turned on, judging by how wet her sex is. Finally we make love, and she has this blissful grin, her brown eyes sparkling, her hands moving feverishly up and down my back as I move in and out of her – slowly at first, and then more quickly, and she comes quickly, bucking against me with some urgency. Her sparkling eyes close and her mouth opens wide as she comes, coming hard, and also trying hard not to make too much noise that might be heard by her housemates...and I'm coming hard myself now, and trying hard to keep my own noise down - although I want to let it all out as much as I'm sure she does. And then we lie there a long time, listening to the music, stroking each other affectionately, and even dozing off for a while.

Suddenly Bea wakes with a start, looks at the alarm clock on the bedside cabinet and exclaims 'Shit, it's half-past four. I've got to go to work!' She gives me a kiss and then starts quickly getting changed into her work clothes – a pair of walking trousers and the usual navy-blue polo tee-shirt with the YHA logo on it; also socks and trainers and a fleece jacket. 'You can stay here for a bit, if you like,' she says, 'but I've got to go now.' She's got to cycle a couple of miles down the valley to the Derwentwater youth hostel, aka 'Barrow House', and she starts work at 4.45pm. I get dressed myself and follow her downstairs and out the back door into the yard, where she keeps her bike. And then we have a parting kiss and I go back into the kitchen to wash up our lunchtime crockery and cutlery and put the kettle on for a cup of tea. But it feels a bit strange hanging around this house so I don't hang around for long and I grab my rucksack, lock the door behind me, get in the car and head back to Rigg Beck.

your way, my way, the way

It's a beautiful sunny day in late-May and I'm loading up the car with all my gear. Rather than take it down the basement staircase, past Mrs Vee's quarters and out through the back door, I've been piling it up in the Blue Room (fortunately unlocked) on the ground floor at the front of the house, and then taking it out through the sash window, which I've got propped wide open with a stick (the sash cord having broken a long time ago). The old purple-painted bench used to be below this window, but someone stole it a year or so ago. It would have been useful right now for stepping onto as I climb in and out of the window, but I can manage without it, balancing boxes and bags on the windowsill and then carrying them the short distance to the car. I've already taken one load to the campsite this morning and piled it up in my new home – the mouldy caravan. This second load will be the last, and I'm thinking that I need to reduce my possessions down to one car load. I could manage with one load, were it not for my desk (which comes apart) and chair, the oil-filled radiator and my bicycle. But these items are very useful, wherever I go, and I'm not going to leave them behind. If I leave anything behind here I might as well say goodbye to it. I suppose I could've asked Mrs Vee to open the front door for me to make this job easier, but I don't really want to ask her anything, besides which she'd probably say 'no'. I'll go and see her with the key to the flat when I'm ready to go, and then that will be it – goodbye Mrs Vee and goodbye Rigg Beck.

Once I've got my final bits into the car I close the Blue Room window and set off for a stroll down the lane to Newlands Church. I love this time of the year when everything is very green – the leaves on the trees and the grass in the fields and on the fells. It's the start of the summer and the sun is shining out of a clear blue sky and the lambs are running and jumping about in the fields, and it's good to be alive today in this particularly beautiful corner of the Lake District.

The lane goes over a bridge at Newlands Beck, and I can see the old gypsy caravan in a secluded spot in a field. I'm not sure, but I think this caravan used to belong to Mrs Vee and used to be parked up at the bottom of the garden at Rigg Beck. Moving on, I turn right up the lane that leads to the church, go through the church gate and look around the little graveyard. I stop at a small headstone that marks the grave of one of Varya's children, who died young. Someone has tried to obliterate the original family name of 'Vergauwen' by crudely daubing the new surname of 'Vee' in red paint over the top of it. But the original surname is still visible underneath. It looks like someone has also tried to deface the carved letters with a chisel or something, but without much success. The original surname is still there, for all to see. It's a name that Varya tried to bury years ago, but it's still there, indestructibly carved into stone, irrefutable evidence to remind her and haunt her. She's never used that old name since I've known her, and it's some kind of taboo to mention it in her presence. Someone once told me that she changed her name when this child died. They said there was some story that made the national papers about the death of the child. There's a small tree growing behind the headstone with its branches bent over the grave like a pair of gnarled old hands strangling some invisible young neck. And there's something scary, something sinister about this grave.

I walk away and go into the little church and sit down on a pew at the back. It's surprisingly cool in here, after the warmth of the sun outside. I close my eyes and try to meditate. My mind turns to Bea. We've been seeing each other for just a week now and we've met up nearly every day and it's going well so far, except that she's already said that she's wary of getting too seriously involved with me as she's moving back to Manchester in September and probably going back to uni, so I don't know how long it's going to last between us – perhaps just for the summer. When we made love in her room yesterday, after we came her eyes welled up with tears and when I asked her 'What's the matter?' her broken voice said 'a surfeit of emotion'. She held back her tears with this cold explanation, not wanting to let go and show her emotion. How beautiful it would have been if she'd been less guarded and burst into tears – I would have loved her for it. But I guess she doesn't want to fall in love with me because it might mess up her career plans. Although she's obviously attracted to me and fond of me, I guess I don't 'tick the boxes' for what she wants on a practical worldly level. I remember when I knew her as just a friend last year she said to me something about my seeming to be 'lost', which annoyed me. I said I wasn't 'lost' because I'd found my vocation and I knew exactly what I wanted to be doing (which was getting stuck into my writing), but that external things (the lack of money and the need to work lots of hours in a menial job) prevented me from doing it. Of course she replied that 'everything is generated *internally*' – one of those seductive new agey ideas to which I have succumbed myself from time to time. And I am reminded of that prayer: 'God grant me the serenity to accept the things I cannot change, the courage to change the things I can, and the wisdom to know the difference.' Some aspects of your reality can be self-created, and others *can't*. And the writing path I have chosen is difficult because it goes against the grain of Main Street and some of those things that cannot be changed. Not just the writing – which I suppose is secondary – but *the way I am* is at odds with the mainstream.

Back outside I'm blinking in the strong sunlight. It's such a fantastic view from here of the Newlands fells

– Hindscarth and Robinson and Dale Head, and the long ridge of Maiden Moor leading to Cat Bells. This is truly paradise, a beautiful place that puts me in mind of 'God' more than the cold musty interior of the church. I walk back over the narrow bridge over the beck and up the lane to the Purple House – still standing as a defiant beacon of alternativeness to Main Street. It's seen better days but it's still there, and I'm glad it's still standing. Before I get to the house there's a broken-down dry-stone wall bordering the bottom part of the garden. I step over this and walk through the overgrown weeds and through the doorway of a tumbledown stone outhouse. In here there's an old iron bed frame and some bits of broken furniture and an old iron fingerpost that presumably once stood at the junction at the top of this lane. At one end of the long metal tube are the three oblong cast iron pointers indicating the directions to three different places. Originally I guess it would have said 'Buttermere', 'Braithwaite' and 'Little Town' (like the current signpost), but at one time in the history of this place some wit has painted over these words with 'HERE', 'THERE' and 'EVERYWHERE', and on the other side: 'YOUR WAY', 'MY WAY' and 'THE WAY'. It makes me smile. It's just the sort of thing that a resident of the Purple House would do.

And then I walk up the final stretch of lane towards the junction, with the house on my right. I'll go and see Mrs Vee with the flat key now. I don't think I'll sign the visitors' book on this occasion; she may not ask me to anyway. It's not exactly been the happiest of my three stays here. I go through the gate into the garden and through the back door, and then I knock on the door to the kitchen and call out her name – 'Mrs Vee!' – but there's no reply. I turn the doorknob and open the door slowly. I am greeted by a 'miaow' as her skinny white cat, which has one green eye and one red eye, slinks past me into the corridor. It's warm in here from the Aga and it has the distinctive old lady odour. High up in a window on the other side is a bright yellow sticker, a representation of a sunburst, through which the actual sun is shining – like a stained glass window. I call out the old lady's name again, but there's no answer. She must have gone into town shopping or something. There's a notepad and pen on the kitchen table and so I write on here, *Varya, here's the flat key, Sol*, and leave the key on the notepad. I close the door behind me and go back into the garden, where the white cat looks up at me as if it's trying to tell me something.

Walking out through the garden gate and back round the front of the house to my loaded-up car, I'm glad that I'm leaving this place, but also sad. It's been good for me in some ways over the years, and it's been an inspiration. But I get the feeling that my personal Purple House history is over now, and that the history of the house itself is nearly over. I get in the car and set off down the road.